A SKULK
OF FOXES

Tales of the City
3

A Skulk of Foxes

A Tale of Magick & the City

Michael Summerleigh

Dancing Wolf Press

Copyright 2024 by Michael Summerleigh
Revised & corrected – October 202r
Design by Michael Summerleigh
Floral borders by David Oxley (UK
Dancing Wolf logo by L.S. Madden, SeeShell Graphics
with inspiration from a design by DansuDragon (UK
Dancing Wolf Press
P.O. Box 194
Tamworth, Ontario
Canada K0k 3G0

with large amounts of thanks for inspiration to
Abe Merritt
Catherine Moore
Jack Vance
Robert Chambers
& J.R.R

A SKULK
OF FOXES

Prologue

THROUGH THE WALL OF SLEEP

He had never seen a desert except in his dreams, but when he consciously sought to go back he knew exactly what it was, and where he was, and how he hoped it would be. He stood in the middle of a broad empty nowhere filled with nothing but sand gone gold and silver in the blistering heat of an equatorial afternoon.

He walked away from the sun, as he had done before, though in front of him again rose up an immense mass of simmering sand shifting in a breeze come straight from the lowest level of Vulcan's basement. That he was stark bare-ass naked didn't trouble him in the least, because it had not been a problem the first time, nor all the other times before the source of his dreaming became apparent, and found its way into his own world. This time he would happily have blistered and died, if only he could find what he was looking for at the end of his search. Desperaton and a sudden sense of his immeasurable loss had brought him back, and as he trudged up the side of the dune, once again found himself overlooking the broad basin similar to the one he'd left behind, he leapt eagerly forward down its face to where the ribbon of sun-struck diamonds ran past it, whispered to the ancient city on the other side...

MICHAEL SUMMERLEIGH

This time there were no foxes to greet him. He imagined them as they had been, at least a score of them, slinking and weaving their way through the sand, always with their noses pointed in his direction and their eyes bright with the curious and somewhat unnerving awareness of the miracle awaiting him.

One of them had been especially curious, and far less wary of him than the others. This one had come to within a dozen paces of him and—in some odd but perfectly logical-seeming way—had herded him in a specific direction every time he went stumbling off a direct route to the river below. This one had glowed in the sunlight, sparks of copper in his rust-red coat, the dark flicker at the end of his tail.

He had felt compelled to follow him, even as what lay below seemed to swim in his sight and become a series of overlapping kaleidoscopic images that encompassed the city glistening in the shimmer of a desert mirage, along with what had felt like an auditory collage of movement, the sound of bare feet skipping along marble hallways, voices lifted in laughter, and songs sung in languages long gone from the earth. This time there was only silence.

As his foxy entourage had led him down to the river, he had found the small coracle woven from the reeds lining the water, that appeared to be there waiting just for him. He had steadied the small boat with his hands as he'd crept into it. The dog-fox had been there…waiting…his button eyes gleaming…his nose and whiskers twitching over what he swore had been a grin…

Now he stepped gingerly from his craft, onto a small wooden quay thrust politely into the slow stream of the river's pilgrimage to the sea, wherever and whatever it might be. From

A SKULK OF FOXES

there he strode again along the broad boulevard of interlocking sandstone pavers that varied in shades of rose and pink to pale almost white, bleached in the sun. Before him rose up the seemingly endless arcade flanked by pillars crowned with the images of every living creature imaginable...

Magically, as before, he had acquired long flowing robes of some silken white cloth through the fibres of which came a soft breeze off the river, redolent with the scents of spice and the promise of secrets revealed and wishes come true. He stopped briefly, thought to hear the faint echo of voices accompanying him, and the strains of musical instruments—a quiet thrumming of *tars*, the twang of single-stringed *rababas*, the lilting rhythms of *ouds* and *kissars*...but it was not real, not even in dream-seeming. Now there was only the silence.

The dog-fox had led him on, loping ahead of him, stopping to look over his shoulder when he had lagged behind. As he had walked along the arcade, shaded now as well by tall date palms and fronded greenery that lifted up large white flowers with crimson hearts that dipped down to shower his way with sweet perfume, he imagined it all as it had been—glimpses of bare-legged serving girls in glowing white *chitons*, brief trills of laughter, the hint of something invisible, long gone but waiting to be reborn. Now there was only the silence.

He walked beneath an arched entryway, flanked by images of fox and leaf, walls painted in arabesques of deep blue, crimson and gold, sandstone giving way to glazed mosaic floors, tapestried walls, furnishings of intricately-carved cedar and rosewood. He sank into a scrolled armchair, found a small tabouret beside him, a ewer and crystal goblet beside it, inviting him to drink.

MICHAEL SUMMERLEIGH

The water was icy cold...sweet...dizzying...

Once again he had come to the palace, cool in spite of the heat outside, forever echoing with intimations of what might have lived and breathed in the shelter of its walls. He drained his goblet, poured himself another, intoxicated by its sweetness, but suddenly feeling as though he could not breathe with the hurt of loss and longing in his heart. Once this place had been alive, waiting for him. Now there was only the silence of centuries, and sand sifting noiselessly through an hourglass of Eternity.

He stood again, tugged briefly at the hem of his robes before he left the entrance hall, down a corridor painted with almost-cuneic characters that felt vaguely familiar to him, and figures that told a story of some sort that he felt certain he had known at one time or another. Suddenly, he heard the soft ghost-like skitter of claws on the marble flooring, following him deeper into the palace...an archway before him filled with nothingness... beckoning...

He thought to hear the faintest whisper of a voice just over his right shoulder...

"Amiri...my prince...NO....!!!!!!"

Part One

LES FANTÔMES DU PASSÉ

Chapter One – A VISITOR FROM THE WEST

"...I thought things would be so different...that they could never be as dreadful as losing her the way we did...and then...Windy, now I miss *her* every bit as much as I missed 'Bella, and it's like I don't even know Gareth anymore..."

They sat downstairs, in the front parlour, the remains of a late lunch before them and the dregs of a pot of coffee, as they sat together with their mugs growing cold and the ongoing stream of Life intruding upon what should have been Peace, and the last fading memories of all the dreadful things that had gone before. Brandywine was wretched, loosed finally from the freely-given promise to a beloved friend, now mired in the consequences and the cost of having survived the avalanche of crises that had come in its wake. Nicholas put his mug on the low table before them, took hers as well, and gathered his wife up where her nearness would allow him to pretend to more optimism than he truly felt.

"Branny you've got t'give all of this more time," he said softly. "I'm sure Zori told Gareth what she intended, and if we'd given it any more thought beyond just our own heart-mending...the joy of getting Arabella back—"

"But I can't bear it, Windy. Can you imagine what it must have been like for him? All of us trooping down t'the ocean to witness a miracle...magick made by the love of his life, at the cost of her own."

"I know..."

"And 'Bella...even without knowing, it's like she *does* know. I'm terrified of what it's gonna do to her when she finds out; that she'll always be thinking she can never be anything more to anyone than a constant reminder that Zori traded her life so she could have hers back."

Nicholas closed his eyes, put his face into her hair and wept in his heart.

"Branny I don't know...I don't have any answers...I know exactly what you're saying, and I love Zori as much as you...but she gave Arabella back to us and honestly... it's dreadful and selfish...but all I can think of is the time we spent without her...and how it was...just horrible..."

She came out from his embrace and straddled his hips where he sat, looking down at him while he refused to look up at her, cradling his head against her chest.

"What're we gonna do, Windy?" she cried softly. "It wasn't supposed t'hurt this much."

"I don't know, honey," he said helplessly. "I just don't know..."

They'd fallen asleep, Brandy somehow again in his arms on the settee, both of them exhausted by all the unresolved confusion come into their lives in the few weeks since their daughter's "return". She raised her head, shook away noontide cobwebs and realised it had been the sound of hooves on the cobblestones of the courtyard of the Mews that had awakened her. She wriggled herself gently from Windy's embrace, kissing him back into wakefulness.

"Someone's here, Windy," she said, and went to the windows of the parlour. "It's a woman...leading a horse..."

He joined her at the windows, saw a slender dark-haired wraith of a woman leading a chestnut mare across the courtyard, of a sudden followed curiously by a swarm of cats, dropping from the apple trees like furry four-footed raindrops. Brandy raced for the front door, flung it wide as the woman stopped a handful of paces away.

"Good morning," said the newcomer, and then, colouring slightly, "Afternoon in truth. I'm looking for the Wyndham house. A man named Alain in the market on Water Street pointed me in this direction. I hope I'm not intruding. My name is Darya Adair..."

She was taller than Brandy by more than four or five inches, lean rather than slender in a leather tunic, riding breeches and boots, a soiled, bell-sleeved white blouse beneath her leathers and an air of great weariness on her sharp-featured face. Dark brown eyes looked at Brandy beseechingly, begging for an end to her journey.

"Alain is family, and you're welcome here," said Brandy, introducing herself. She called back to Nicholas, who joined her a moment later and, without hesitation, stepped forward to relieve the woman of her pack and take the reins of the mare in hand. When the stranger made to introduce herself further, Brandy shook her head and said:

"Come inside first. We'll find something for you t'eat and drink, and everything else can wait until you're comfortable."

A SKULK OF FOXES

Windy was already leading the mare away to the small stable in the rock garden behind the carriage house.

"I don't want t'be any kind of trouble for you," said Darya Adair, taking Brandy's offered hand with a look of infinite gratitude.

"That will never happen," said Brandy. "If Alain sent you, then you've got every right and reason t'be here."

Darya's head went a bit sideways at her words. She began to cry, sparing a glance for Nicholas and the mare clomping round the carriage house and descending into the back garden, and then down to where Brandy held her hand firmly in her own, drawing her through the door of the coach house.

"You don't even know me—"

"I know your name," said Brandy. "My daughter Arabella has spoken of someone named Robin Adair..."

"...He was my husband," said Darya.

They sat in the kitchen, looking out over the rock garden. Nicholas, having sensed that this newcomer to their lives had no need of his immediate presence, had stabled the mare and gone upstairs to the music room, playing an old sonata quietly, leaving Brandy to give welcome.

Her eyes went wide at the pain in her guest's words.

"Was...?"

"It was such a dreadful winter..." said Darya.

Brandy nodded, feeling something coil around her heart and squeeze.

"We sent so much to the City, to help everyone here get through the winter once the Antillians were gone. Robin said it was the right thing t'do, that we could always make do with short days on the ocean to keep us in Bedford fed...

"A handful of boats went out just after the new year, but a storm came up from out of nowhere...and when one of them went down in it, Robin tried to save them that was the crew..."

They wept together, because Sorrow had no boundaries and each of them had come to their own in the days not long past.

"...Rob talked about your daughter all the time...how Arabella had saved his life...given him the best friendships he'd ever known...how they'd promised together he would bring the mare back when everything was over..."

"'Bella only wanted him t'be back safe with you," Brandy said. "She's said that when Robin spoke of you, it was like listening to herself wanting Kerissa...her girl... She never once truly thought he would take their promise to each other seriously..."

Darya watered her tea with tears..

"And he never once gave thought to *not* bringing the mare back to her. I should have come sooner, but the winter was hard, and in the spring, with the gardens and such needing work...and my children..."

Darya began to sob uncontrollably, leaning across the bench beside the table to where Brandy became her sanctuary and solace.

"And this...I didn't want to leave them, I never wanted t'go anywhere ever again...but I got this...from the palace...I remember Rob once said you were somebody important there..."

A SKULK OF FOXES

She reached into her tunic and brought forth an envelope and a summons scripted upon lavender paper in purple ink. Brandy read the commendation...the request that Robin Adair present himself to the court to be rewarded for his service to the realm.

"I was just an assistant, Darya, for a little while...not really important at all...but I'll go with you, I can do that...tomorrow in the morning, maybe? And you can stay here tonight."

"I don't want t'be a bother—"

"Darya we've got lots of room."

"Okay. Tomorrow then. If you could go with me I'd be so grateful. I mean, I have t'go, don't I? I can't just ignore it...and I had t'bring your daughter's pony back...Rob promised..."

And Brandy felt her heart begin to pound, wondering how in the world her daughter was going survive yet another catastrophe come into her life.

❦

She had just finished putting the guest-room in order, with Darya fresh out of a bath, both of them now with Windy downstairs in the kitchen, when the front door on the main floor of the coach-house banged open and a pair of ragamuffins came charging down the stairs.

"Annie Branny we're back!" shouted Stella.

"'Rissa and 'Bella took us t'the fairgrounds and—"

Jamie caught sight of Darya at the the far end of the long table and came to a dead stop behind his twin sister.

"Oh. Hi. Who are you?" he asked with a lot less volume.

Almost eight-year old mop-topped mirror images of each other in shorts and singlets and sandals, they stood together nervously, unused to finding unfamiliar faces in any of their familiar places. Nicholas turned from slicing tomatoes and celery for a recipe he'd found tucked into a libretto from Italia.

"Jamie. Stella. This is Darya. I know we've never spoken of her, but she's part of our family...from Bedford..."

"We've been t'Bedford," said Stella. "Last year, before 'Bella went away. We saw sea monsters..."

"Only one," added Jamie.

"These two belong to Alain on Water Street," explained Brandy. "He and my oldest friend, Andrew, adopted them..."

"We have two dads," Stella said proudly.

Darya closed her eyes for an instant, and her fingers tightened round the new mug of tea on the table in front of her. Then she opened her eyes and smiled.

"I've got two girls I'm sure are the same age as you...they're my twins Devon and Daryl...and my son Daniel. He's the youngest...five years old..."

"Then they're our cousins!" cried Stella. "Maybe when we do holidays again we can meet them...?"

The twins were too young to see the three grown-ups in the room catch themselves up short one breath, suddenly too interested in the prospect of new family to notice the quick exchange of agonised glances, or the grateful breath drawn to their innocent acceptance.

Darya looked down into her mug of tea and smiled again...

"I'm sure that would be the best thing in the world..." she said.

...As Arabella and Kerissa tumbled into the kitchen on their own and did more adult versions of being surprised by the presence of someone they'd never met before.

A SKULK OF FOXES

Windy said, "'Rissa...'Bella...this is Darya Adair... Robin's wife. She's come t'return the mare you sent home with him last year..."

Brandy felt like she'd somehow been transported to a place where every last nightmare in her heart had been given some dreadful kind of life in the look of horrific sadness on her daughter's face. Arabella looked at Darya and Darya looked at Arabella, and the younger woman seemed to simply stop breathing. Brandy could almost watch the thoughts go shredding through the mind of her daughter, who said...

"Oh. Hi. It's so lovely t'meet you, Darya. What happened to Robin?"

...Before she turned and ran back up the stairs, wailing...

Chapter Two – Into the Dark

The twins were too stunned to say or do anything. Brandywine rose instinctively, but Kerissa shook her head *No* and turned to follow Arabella up the stairs, and while Nicholas would have followed her, he encountered Jamie and Stella between him and the door of the kitchen and their looks of terror stopped him dead in his tracks. He knelt in front of them, took them both into his arms and put his head down where Stella had burst into tears on his shoulder.

I know you're scared," he whispered. "I am too, but it's gonna be okay, guys, I promise. I'm gonna take you home now, okay? I know we were all supposed t'have supper here with your das, but it's turned out not t'be a good time so I'm gonna take you home. Are you gonna be okay with that…?"

"What's wrong with 'Bella?" asked Jamie. "I thought she would be so happy t'come home after all that time."

"There's more to it than that, Jamie," soothed Nicholas. "It's taken us all by surprise, I guess."

"'Bella didn't go away, did she?" sobbed Stella.

"What d'you mean, honey?"

"I don't know what I mean, but I'm not stupid, Uncle Nicky. She came back but it's not the same anymore. She's so unhappy…"

A SKULK OF FOXES

Nicholas nodded, kissed the top of her head, and would have done the same for Jamie but for him pulling himself away angrily.

"You're the grown-ups. You're the ones supposed t'take care of all of us!" he shouted. "Why're you letting her hurt so much? She's your baby, why don't you help her?"

Nicholas climbed painfully back to his feet, stricken, looked helplessly at Brandywine and back to the children.

"Okay. You're right, Jamie. Me and Annie Branny haven't been doing our job. Please…let's get you guys home for now, and tonight we'll start on trying t'make things better."

"You have to, Uncle Windy," whispered Stella. "I don't wanna be here if 'Bella goes away again."

There was a moment of complete desolation that he recognised from twenty years before, when the world had come crashing down upon his shoulders, and a strange confluence of Time and Tide that had brought him rescue from the friends he had found in the City.

"Then I'm just gonna have t'find a way t'fix everything for both of you *and* 'Bella," he said. "Come with me now. Let's get your stuff and we'll get you home, and then I'll come back here and try …"

When they were gone, Darya said, "Go look after her, Brandywine. I'll be okay here for a while."

Brandy shook her head.

"No. It's okay. 'Rissa knows her better than anyone…even me… It's been like that forever, since the day Arabella was born. Kerissa just…I don't know…she just took ownership of my little girl. She was here every day…*every day*…and she wasn't even three years old but she knew exactly what t'do when 'Bella cried...or was sick..."

Darya took her hand.

"There's a lot more to my new family than I know about," she said. "I *do* know you'd rather be upstairs with your daughter, but you said she'll be okay with 'Rissa looking after her so tell me... everything...anything...

"For starters, *you're* Annie Branny...?"

Brandy nodded.

"When Alain and Andrew first brought the twins home they were too young t'say Aunt Brandywine...so I became Annie Branny...and all the other kids thought that was funny so..."

"All the other kids...?"

"Tomorrow, Darya...but I guess it really all began a long long time ago..."

"...'Bella's sick!" cried Stella.

They'd decided to walk down to the harbourfront, and then, on Water Street, encountered Alain closing things up for the night. He looked at Windy, who explained, and then said:

"I don't know how we ever believed we could just ignore it all, and hope she wouldn't notice."

Alain could only be described as nothing less than beautiful. He and Andrew might have been brothers, delicately-featured, wide-eyed and so devoid of any of the stupid things that seemed to define being masculine that they might once, when each of them was younger than they were now, have been mistaken for girls...and yet each of them had

A SKULK OF FOXES

proven themselves to be indomitable, and possessed of some kind of ferocity when it came to protecting those whom they loved. Alain leaned towards the man whom he viewed as a saviour of his beloved in the days before they had met, and kissed him. .

"I'll take the children home, bring them to work with me tomorrow," he said. "And I'll make sure Andrew comes to the house in the morning."

"Branny's taking someone t'the palace."

"But you'll be there," said Alain. "And Andy will be along, I'm sure."

Nicholas nodded. "I think I could use the help. Thank you, Alain..."

Alain shook his head. "You don't have t'thank me for anything, Windy. Look after the girls. Andy would die if we lost Arabella again..."

Arabella's bedroom appeared to be empty, which served only to strike at Kerissa's heart that much more dreadfully. She called out her name...softly...to let her know she was there, and waited... waited...waited again...in the silence...before she went to the closet, inched her way past the door into the darkness and found her girl cowering in the corner.

"I'm here...'Bella...I'm here..."

"Go away, 'Rissa! I hate you!"

"Please...please don't ever say that..."

"How could you let them do this t'me?"

"'Bella...can't you see we had no idea what t'do...?"

"Did you think I wouldn't see everybody tippy-toeing around me all over again? Did you think I wouldn't notice that I haven't seen your mom in all the time since I woke up... from sleeping for six months?!?! How did that happen, 'Rissa? You're s'posed t'be the one who loves me more than anyone else in the world..."

" 'Bella please..."

" 'Rissa I fell asleep in the middle of a snowstorm... and then I woke up bare-ass naked on a tapestry floating in off the ocean six months later? What was that all about? Why can't *anyone* look me in the eye and tell me? Why won't *you* tell me...?

"And now I find out Robin is dead? What *else* happened that nobody's talking about when I'm around...?"

"Baby...please..."

"NO! Don't beg me to let you get off without explaining, 'Rissa. I'm so tired. I can't do this anymore. I can't just pretend I'm this cheery stupid blondie after all the things I've done..."

" 'Bella stop it's—"

"It's more than I can deal with, 'Rissa! Don't you know that what I want more than anything else is just t'be naked next to you forever? D'you think I wouldn't give half the world for that? All of it...? What do I have t'do...?"

There was dead silence, the whisper of breath up and in amongst the clothing hanging in Arabella's closet. Kerissa felt her heart breaking in the way that hearts get broken time after time when they find so few answers to make up for the hurt and desolation of being alive. Her fingernails began to shred the wooden floorboards beneath her....

"Help me, 'Rissa...please help me..."

A SKULK OF FOXES

Arabella's hand found hers in the dark and wouldn't let go...

"...And I think that's how it all got started...more than twenty years ago...that night when Windy heard something...felt something in the air and it turned out t'be...well...I guess we've never ever really found out what it was...but we all heard it. And whatever it was that we heard...it was still there for Zori to use against the Antillians..."

Darya poured more tea for both of them, well past surprise or skepticism, but puzzled nevertheless. Brandywine paid attention to the steam rising up off the top of her mug, stirred some honey into it.

"We met Queen Caroline by accident...me and Windy. We became good friends, and then she asked me to take her place..."

"So ever since she died...twenty years ago when all of this began...you've been the one to keep up the illusion she was still alive...?"

"Oh no...I could never have done that, been the queen, but I promised I'd help t'find someone, so she could rest. I said I'd do my best. I said I'd try, and I had lots of help. I could never have done any of it all by myself."

Darya sipped at her own mug, and then reached for Brandywine's hand.

"I find that difficult to believe."

"Well it doesn't matter anymore, Darya. Now it's just about 'Bella...and poor Gareth...'Rissa's father..."

"Can I ask what happened to Arabella...?"

MICHAEL SUMMERLEIGH

Brandy nodded into her tea, weighing how much she could say, without betraying a confidence from half a lifetime ago.

"It was before Yule-tide. Once the Antillians were gone we thought all the horrible things were over and done with, but the one who had started the whole mess for us—plotted with Antillia, roused the Scandians, fired the plot to take over the throne—was still alive, and he came for Zoraya. My little girl killed him and saved Zori's life, but she had to go over a cliff with him t'do it. We thought she'd been killed…

"Once Zori was recovered, she started asking about 'Bella and I told her what had happened…and then she said there was something she might be able t'do. She never said what it was, but then suddenly, just a few weeks ago, 'Bella found her way back to us…it was like magick…but Zori was gone…"

They heard footsteps on the stairs…quiet …then more footsteps, descending the flight into the kitchen. Kerissa in tears.

"She was in hiding her closet. She doesn't remember anything that happened and now she hates all of us because she doesn't know…doesn't know what to feel about anything because no one will tell her, and I'm afraid what will happen if I do. I have t'go home. My da is all by himself…"

Brandy reached out to her, was on her feet and rushing towards her, but Kerissa already had turned and flung herself back up the stairs.

"I hate this…someone please make it stop…"

When Nicholas returned from Water Street he found his wife in the arms of the woman from Bedford. He put his arms around both of them.

Chapter Three - Old Princes Street

Kerissa fled down the Boulevard in tears, oblivious to the horse-drawn carts and motor-cars that narrowly missed her as she crossed before them in flagrant disregard of all the given rules. She ran blindly, in pain, and for the first time in all the years she had been in love with Arabella, wounded by her desperation, doubting her ability to unravel the utter contempt her girl felt for herself, or the anger that drove her to turn on those who loved her..

When she reached the studio on Old Princes Street it was almost dark; she had to fumble in the pockets of her trousers to find the key to the small door set into the wide doors of what had been a stable before it had become her father's studio. Inside there was only the deepening shadows of evening rushing into nightfall. And silence. The undeniable total absence of sound made by living things...

"Da...?" she called.

And there was silence.

She fumbled in the mirk drifting up from the floorboards...found scratch-matches on a work-table...wandered the ground floor until every last lamp and candle had been lit and the flickering light fighting her own desperate terror to come to terms with something she felt had no way of having a positive outcome.

She called out... "Daddy...?" ...and received no answer...waiting and waiting and then climbing the stairs to the gallery walks overlooking the studio space below. Nowhere could she find evidence of her father having been there that day. She retraced her steps, extinguishing all the lamps and candles, and then climbed back upstairs, to her own bedroom and the chaotic tumble of her twenty-year old existence... clothing flung in every direction...her bed linens all over everywhere, still sweet with memory of the last time Bella had stayed the night...

Kerissa said *Fuck!* and buried herself in the sheets, finding Arabella in every fold and crease, inhaling the scent of her, some small measure of comfort in her absence.

It was throughly dark when she awoke. She rose and re-lit a lamp, took another tour of the upstairs rooms and again found no indication that her father had spent any time in any of them while she slept. In her mother's workroom, she pulled a handful of threads from the loom that had been idle for almost a month, and wept because she had yet to find any way out of the nightmare that had come to live with Arabella. She dragged herself back into her own room...went to a chest of drawers and drew out a small rectangular box of dark cedar, hinged and bound in silver arabesques, inlaid with ebony and ivory... drew out a handful of what she knew were sheets of ancient papyrus, somehow having survived centuries to receive the last words from her mother:

ZORAYA'S LETTER
My dearest daughter Kerissa

A SKULK OF FOXES

I don't know when you will find this. I hope it will be soon, so you will know why I am gone from you, and your father, who will forever be the love of my life.

I have forgotten a great many things since you and Arabella saved me from Chakidze.

My sense of Time—always somewhat wonky (?) for reasons I imagine you can surmise and (hopefully) laugh at—has not served me well in these last few months when you and Brandywine and everyone in our family looked after me.

But I remember what is important, my beautiful baby. I remember being a child and having parents with great hopes and ambitions for me; and I remember growing up almost alone while they pursued the best interests of the family into which I was born so long ago, and sought to ensure my place in it as one of honour and high station. And I also remember the path I chose and how I was lost to them when younger even than you.

I know there is the greatest possibility you will hate me for abandoning you and your father, but I once told him I was just a visitor in this new world, the one into which he brought me, all unknowing, because I had willed him to do so.

And then I became lost in the shower of Love he rained upon me, a parched child of the desert, and it has been the most wonderful time in all of the time I spent living and trying to survive in the midst of nowhere. And in all of that, he gave me you...

I have no words, my sweet girl, to tell you how much you have meant to me...to convey how much joy and wonder you have brought to the dull magicks of my own too-lengthy existence. And when I saw Arabella for the first time...with you beside me...and how suddenly you became this exquisite little creature dedicated to the small helpless thing Brandywine had brought into the world...

I knew then that I had found the true reason for being returned to Life; that your father and I were to be for you the parents I had never known; that you and your 'Bella were what was meant to be, to go on in the world; that together, you and she would have so much more to offer our friends and our family and all the living things I would never encounter as a result of my small richly-rewarded selfish act of resurrection.

I've told your father what I intend. I've tried to make him understand that I would not have survived if not for you...if not for Arabella. I would have been lost to him, as I have chosen to become lost to him now. But being who he is, your father has understood what I was trying to tell him.

You are the one who is important, my love. You and your happiness...and that of the girl you love...who saved my life at the cost of her own...

Your father and I have chosen to give her back to you. Never...please...never regret what I have done. You will see me in her eyes for as long as she can look at you. You must help her to understand...and you must love her forever, as I will always love you and my precious Gareth.

What I did was something that had never been done before, 'Rissa. Bringing Arabella back to you may have more consequences than I know of, so be wary and always keep the gift I've left you close by.

I can no longer see into the past or the future, so I will leave both to your care.

A SKULK OF FOXES

I love you, my little girl. Someday I hope we will see each other again and I will kiss your eyes and feel your heart beating Love into mine...

Take care of them...take care of all of them...

She folded the brittle pages carefully, and laid them down flat in the bottom of her treasure box, beneath the trinkets and beads...a lock of 'Bella's hair from when she was a baby...a small handful of photographs... She leafed through the pages of a tiny picture book of fairy tales...pressed a toy bracelet seven-year old Arabella had given her on her tenth birthday to her cheek...

Then she took the ring up, cupped it in her hands—a moonstone set in silver—slipped it onto the forefinger of her left hand, where it fit perfectly. She took a long deep breath and gathered up every bit of strength she could muster for the storm she knew was coming, before exhaustion once again drove her into sleep...

※

When she awoke, shivering, she realised that somehow she was no longer in her own bed; that there was grass beneath one of her outflung hands, damp and cold and black in the stream of moonlight that filtered through the stand of trees atop the hill above her. She turned, totally disoriented, until she saw a vast shadow not far beyond the dying embers of the campfire had been set beside her...she thought...

I know this place. I know that horse.

...And slowly crawled from beneath the thin blanket she shared with Arabella, softly calling out...

Diomede.

...Stifling a scream...

Don't wake Arabella.

...As the massive shadow of a head turned to her and she saw the blank empty spaces...

Empty spaces...in the dark...?

...Where the draft horse's eyes should have been, and the smoulder of something rising up from the ground where its hooves met the earth. Instinctively, she reached for the long dagger on her belt but it was gone, along with the rest of her clothing; that she was naked and defenseless as the horse moved towards her, hellfire curling from its nostrils in ribbons of smoke and blood. She forced herself to stand her ground, calling out to wake Arabella...taking a precious instant to kneel beside where she should have been...

'Bella where are you?

...Searching desperately for her in the moonlight, knowing now exactly where she was and that it was a thorough impossibility for her to be...

In the Westvales, months ago...Bella where are you answer me please.

...As the thing that was not Diomede made dreadful sounds in its throat and moved towards her with its absence of eyes blazing. She turned and ran, seeking the higher ground of the hillside as a small measure of advantage against whatever was following her, stumbling to her knees where the grass felt like snakes wriggling up her inner thighs...crawling...on her feet again as she came to the crest of the hill, thought to find some kind of defense or shelter in the stand of trees.

With the prescient horror of Memory being transformed into Nightmare, she saw the body with five arrows in its back,

A SKULK OF FOXES

pinning it to the foremost tree-trunk, as it squirmed and tore itself loose through the fletching of each arrow...one by one...before it turned... collapsed at her feet, reaching for her with hands gone to shredded flesh and bare bone.

It smiled up at her...gleefully...another impossibility with so little left of his face...Renard de Montenay said:

"I'm not done with you *or* your slut, *afrique*...not by a long shot..."

※

When she awoke in the darkness before the dawn, shivering, she sensed something had changed; that she was no longer alone in the loft above her father's studio on Old Princes Street. She crept cautiously out onto the gallery, trembling, still in the toils of the dream, went the length of it to her parents' bedroom hoping her father had come home while she had slept; but the bed was neatly made, had not been slept in, and she realised she was afraid to call out to him, afraid of the almost suffocating silence that seemed to have grown deeper while she slept.

She turned back, moving slowly towards the downstairs, and realised something else was waiting for her...that the floor of the studio seemed to be moving like an ocean tide in the flood of a desert sunset, filled with shapeless things that seemed to mew and cry and struggle as they crawled through the haze.

She closed her eyes and leapt from the stairs, went knee-deep into the mist, gratefully felt her feet strike upon wooden floorboards as she raced through the studio. At the door to the street she turned, saw the shadows coming for her, slammed it shut behind her and ran...

Chapter Four - Reckonings

Brandywine looked up from her mug of coffee, found Darya standing in the doorway already dressed in a skirt of some soft brown fabric with a matching short-waisted jacket, a wide-collared shirt of bleached white linen, and plain sandals on her feet.

"I couldn't sleep. I've been awake for hours, just staring up into the dark. I hope this is okay for going t'the palace. It's all I've got in the way of dress-up."

Brandy went to the stove and poured a second mug for her, added some cream and a spoon of honey, turned to her guest.

"You look perfectly wonderful," she said, smiling ruefully, "and you should've come looking for me we could've kept each other company. I spent some time just sittin' beside 'Bella; then I went back t'bed and Windy was like a log so I've been wandering around waiting for everyone t'wake up and trying not t'make too much noise."

Darya's answering smile was a cautious one, gratefully accepting her coffee, turning her gaze to the first bits of daylight creeping into the back garden.

"It's lovely here. Once upon a time my little house in Bedford was lovely too...until the storm..."

"I never said how sorry I was, even though I never met Robin."

A SKULK OF FOXES

Darya looked away, scrubbed her face with a sleeve. "I don't know if I'm ever gonna be comfortable with him being gone, but I suppose you've felt that way too."

Brandy nodded. "You've got somebody lookin' after the children?"

"My folks. Robin's mom. They've been so good...but sometimes I feel like such a rotten person because as much as I miss him...you know...all the small silly things we shared every day...it's night-time that's the worst, him not being there...and sometimes I just wish *somebody* was there, so I wasn't just reaching out into this empty place where he used t'be...

"I guess that doesn't make any sense..."

Brandy sighed, looked out into the garden.

"It makes plenty of sense, Darya. I think it's because when you can't bear t'have lost someone who's been the world t'you, there's this little place inside where the hurt makes you stupid for anything that even feels a little bit like it used t'be.

"For six months I was just lucky to have Windy and my best friend Andrew... everyone in our family. I don't know how it would've been if 'Bella had not found her way back to us...but I guess it's never gonna be the same for you, is it?"

Darya shook her head, unwilling to look Brandy in the eye.

"And now you're wishin' for the same kind of miracle to bring Robin back..."

"I am. It's so selfish. I don't even know Arabella...but today we're going to the palace so the brand new king can tell me how much all of us owe my dead husband."

MICHAEL SUMMERLEIGH

Nicholas was in the upstairs music room, with coffee and the beginnings of a nocturne on the sheet of staff paper on his piano, when he heard his front door open and close quietly, followed by footsteps on the stairs. A moment later, Andrew appeared and Nicholas rose to greet him, leaning into the offered hand that came to brush his cheek.

"Thanks for coming, Andy. I don't know what t'do with Arabella anymore. We had so many talks last year when I offered up anything I could think of t'help her deal with all the horrible things she'd gone through. Now I have no idea what t'say."

Andrew took him by the shoulders, his dark eyes bright with resolve.

"Alain told me what you said yesterday and I thought about it all night...so *I'm* going t'tell her, Windy," he said quietly. "She's always been willing t'talk with and listen t'me, and I've never been one t'bring any kind of discord into her life. When she realised that her relationship with 'Rissa went far deeper than just being children together, she came t'me to ask if what she was feeling was wrong, and I told her about my experience with Father Ambrosius, the night I spent in the crypt beneath the church, and how the most important things I've learned in my life have come from Branny and you and Alain... about trusting the people who trust you..."

Nicholas shook his head in relief and disbelief all at the same time.

"Are you sure, Andy? This is so far beyond all of the things she's ever had t'deal with....and she's going t'feel even worse when she finds out what Zori did..."

A SKULK OF FOXES

"Alain thinks it's the right thing t'do," said Andrew. "He's never wrong about stuff like that. Is she awake yet?"

Windy nodded. "She's still in bed, but I'm pretty sure she's up. I've been here so I could be close by, but I've heard her moving around some..."

"Okay then," said Andrew. "I'm on my way wish me luck."

"Good luck, Andy...I love you..."

"Me too you, Nicholas. I'll do the best I can for our girl."

Andrew walked slowly to the bedroom door halfway down the upper hall, knocked softly and waited.

"Go away!"

"'Bella it's me...Andrew..."

There was what felt like an endless and painful silence before he heard footsteps padding toward the door; when it opened slowly, Arabella was in a flannel nightgown to her knees and stockinged feet, her hair a mare's-nest of tangles, emerald eyes dull with exhaustion and her face haggard from lack of sleep.

"Uncle Andrew please—"

"No, 'Bella. You know how much you mean t'me and it's about time you had the answers t'all your questions."

"'Rissa should have said. My mom and dad..."

"They didn't know what t'say, 'Bella. Please...let me be the one t'tell you what you want t'know."

"I don't want to hate you, Uncle Andrew!"

"And I want you t'see all of this has nothing t'do with Hate and everything t'do with how much we love you."

For a moment he imagined her as she stood before him now, but years and years past, when she was younger even than the twins. She took a tangled twist of hair between her fingers and began to cry, standing back from the door as he slipped through and closed it behind him. Andrew had a handkerchief.

"Why don't you get back under the covers, honey," he said, offering it. "You don't have t'say anything if you don't want to."

For Andrew it was like watching his oldest friend in agony. Arabella was nothing if not Brandywine's daughter, and her misery was something akin to the misery had been in his own heart when Brandy first had found him sleeping in an alleyway that since had been obliterated under the onslaught of the Antillian armada. Arabella climbed back onto her bed, crept beneath her blankets and pulled them up to her chin. Andrew perched himself at the end of the bed.

"D'you remember anything at all, 'Bella?" he asked.

She shrugged. "I don't know if it's remembering for real. I don't *know* anything anymore."

"Tell me...the day you fell asleep..."

"I didn't fall asleep!"

Andrew put his head down.

"I know," he said.

"Then don't say it anymore, Uncle Andrew. I know it's not true. I don't know what happened, but I *do* know I didn't fall asleep.

"Me and 'Rissa were going shopping...I think that's what we were gonna do. We went outside and out of nowhere Hasan jumped into her arms." She stopped as something else came along to savage her heart. "Andrew where's Hasan?"

Andrew reached for her, stopped as she cringed away from him. From the day she had come back, there had been sparks of gold in her green eyes, sparks that in the course of a few weeks

A SKULK OF FOXES

"Alain thinks it's the right thing t'do," said Andrew. "He's never wrong about stuff like that. Is she awake yet?"

Windy nodded. "She's still in bed, but I'm pretty sure she's up. I've been here so I could be close by, but I've heard her moving around some..."

"Okay then," said Andrew. "I'm on my way wish me luck."

"Good luck, Andy...I love you..."

"Me too you, Nicholas. I'll do the best I can for our girl."

Andrew walked slowly to the bedroom door halfway down the upper hall, knocked softly and waited.

"Go away!"

"'Bella it's me...Andrew..."

There was what felt like an endless and painful silence before he heard footsteps padding toward the door; when it opened slowly, Arabella was in a flannel nightgown to her knees and stockinged feet, her hair a mare's-nest of tangles, emerald eyes dull with exhaustion and her face haggard from lack of sleep.

"Uncle Andrew please—"

"No, 'Bella. You know how much you mean t'me and it's about time you had the answers t'all your questions."

"'Rissa should have said. My mom and dad..."

"They didn't know what t'say, 'Bella. Please...let me be the one t'tell you what you want t'know."

"I don't want to hate you, Uncle Andrew!"

"And I want you t'see all of this has nothing t'do with Hate and everything t'do with how much we love you."

For a moment he imagined her as she stood before him now, but years and years past, when she was younger even than the twins. She took a tangled twist of hair between her fingers and began to cry, standing back from the door as he slipped through and closed it behind him. Andrew had a handkerchief.

"Why don't you get back under the covers, honey," he said, offering it. "You don't have t'say anything if you don't want to."

For Andrew it was like watching his oldest friend in agony. Arabella was nothing if not Brandywine's daughter, and her misery was something akin to the misery had been in his own heart when Brandy first had found him sleeping in an alleyway that since had been obliterated under the onslaught of the Antillian armada. Arabella climbed back onto her bed, crept beneath her blankets and pulled them up to her chin. Andrew perched himself at the end of the bed.

"D'you remember anything at all, 'Bella?" he asked.

She shrugged. "I don't know if it's remembering for real. I don't *know* anything anymore."

"Tell me...the day you fell asleep..."

"I didn't fall asleep!"

Andrew put his head down.

"I know," he said.

"Then don't say it anymore, Uncle Andrew. I know it's not true. I don't know what happened, but I *do* know I didn't fall asleep.

"Me and 'Rissa were going shopping...I think that's what we were gonna do. We went outside and out of nowhere Hasan jumped into her arms." She stopped as something else came along to savage her heart. "Andrew where's Hasan?"

Andrew reached for her, stopped as she cringed away from him. From the day she had come back, there had been sparks of gold in her green eyes, sparks that in the course of a few weeks had gone dull and glazed with her hurt. Suddenly they were back... blazing...

"Where is he?"

Andrew looked away for a moment, drew a deep breath, and looked into them.

"Hasan's dead, 'Bella. 'Rissa told us what happened. She didn't know how to tell you any more than the rest of us. Hasan died...*and so did you*...."

He didn't know what frightened him more—the look of dumb surprise that swept over her beautiful face, or the re-doubled fire in her eyes that came back in disbelief and horror as a comprehension of what he'd said sank in.

"I'm dead?"

"No, 'Bella, you're not. You were...gone...for a while...but then you came back..."

And Andrew told her everything that Kerissa had told him—how the creature that was Chakidze...Azim Sharad...the sorcerer who had roused two invasions from abroad and an insurrection at home, for no other reason than to wreak revenge upon Kerissa's mother for a centuries-old grievance, finally had come to inflict that vengeance upon her on the headlands overlooking the ocean west of Bedford...

"...Hasan found you and 'Rissa outside your door, here in the Mews. You ran upstairs, dragged your swordbelt from the closet, wrapped yourself around them both and in moments... somehow...found yourselves on the high street in Bedford. You got horses from the owner of the Moonstruck Mermaid and arrived on the headlands in time to see Zoraya struck down...

"Kerissa went to her mother. *You* went for the sorcerer. Hasan leapt at him, and was clawed to death. You came an instant later on horseback...leapt at him yourself... drove a dagger up into his brain and went over the cliff with him...

"You saved her life, 'Bella. You saved us all. If that creature had survived, there's no way of knowing what he would have done to us..."

"I'm dead."

"No, 'Bella, you're not dead. You're alive. It truly doesn't matter how...but you're back here...with everyone who loves you."

"That's not possible. Not if I was dead."

Andrew realised he had come to the part of his tale where the sanity of his beloved friend's daughter hung in the balance.

"'Bella listen...listen closely...please... You know Zoraya was magick; that the mere fact of her existence among us was something only t'be dreamt of...fairy tales...the absence of all the things that most of us believe in order t'keep our worlds in perfect order.

"When Zoraya finally was well enough to get up from her bed in the aftermath of her encounter with Chakidze, your mother asked her to destroy the amaranth, the unfading flower that had bestowed a longer-than-normal lifespan to those of the de Montigny dynasty, and untrammeled power to someone who might know the truth of it. That much I know you remember, how it allowed Zoraya to save the kingdom from the Antillian fleet. But your mother felt that in light of all the things that had happened, it had the potential to do more harm than any more lasting good. She begged Zoraya to destroy it, and Zoraya begged your mother to trust her one last time, and not to ask any questions...

A SKULK OF FOXES

" 'Bella, she would have died if not for you. And then she *chose* to give you back to us...to the girl who loves you...her own daughter, Kerissa...

"In destroying the amaranth, she took the last of its own dying existence...and the life Kerissa's father had given back to her...so you could be with us again..."

Kerissa sprinted, ran as she'd never run in her life, tattering her sandals, kicking them loose all uncaring that her feet began to blister on the paved sidewalks of the Boulevard.

As she drew near to the Café of the Silver Rose she saw a familiar face, darted in and out of the rush of morning traffic, heedless of the horns and outraged shouts in her wake. She threw herself into welcoming arms and fought for breath enough to speak.

" 'Rissa...?"

"Just for a minute, Annie Branny...I gotta go..."

Brandywine turned to Darya in confusion, caught the girl up in her arms before she fell to her knees.

"My da's gone, Branny! He didn't come home last night and I had this horrible dream and the studio's all full of I don't know what kind of weird stuff. Everything's gone funny peculiar and I got this big wiggins goin' on, but I have t'see 'Bella first... before anything else...tell her the truth..."

" 'Rissa, we have t'go t'the palace..."

"Okay but come home soon, please come home soon..."

"Okay we will, but don't say anything t'Bella until we get back...?"

But Kerissa was already gone, Brandywine and Darya watching her race past the terrace of the Silver Rose on her way to the coach house in St John's Mews.

"That didn't sound good," said Darya.

Brandy said, "No, not at all..." and in answer to the Bedford woman's puzzlement, "Windy's there, and he said Andy would be coming this morning..."

"Should we go back?"

"Brandy shook her head. "No...you need t'go...and there's people who need t'see you even if they don't know it yet."

Darya started shaking.

"Brandy I don't think I can do this."

"Of course you can. You'll be okay, I promise. I'll make sure..."

"Brandy...?"

She had to reach up a bit, but she took Darya's face in both her hands, kissed her, and smiled.

"What about...Kerissa...and your daughter?"

Brandy sighed.. "I guess we'll deal with whatever that is when we get back..."

Kerissa had to stop running, the pavement shredding the soles of her feet. As she limped past the Church of St John the Defender, down the cobbled entrance to the Mews and past the door of the artist who once upon a time had been Aengus Robertson to the rest of the world, she stopped to catch her breath, and then to sob as she saw the roil of whatever it was that had chased her from Old Princes Street, obscuring the courtyard, barring her path to the door of the Wyndham house.

It was like looking out over a small lake whereon some mad artist-god had decided to marble-ise the heavens by swirling oil and paint upon the surface of the water, that it might be reflected up to adorn the sky. She hesitated, found dozens of cats and catlings peering out wide-eyed and curious from the new foliage of the apple trees that ringed the courtyard. As she watched the surge and swirl of the strangeness unfolding upon the ground, she heard the soft pad of something coming up behind her on the cobblestones of the laneway, turned to find a doglike creature come to sit patiently staring at her less than a breath from her heels.

A scratchy small voice whispered in her head. She heard a name...*Thelina*...and in it the memory of a night of horror in the Westvales...a night of flight upon the moors of the Carillon... and a bitch-fox who had served her and Arabella upon both occasions.

"It *was* you," breathed Kerissa.

The vixen dipped her muzzle once, seemed almost to smile, but with a deep sadness underlying the welcome of Kerissa's recognition. The whisper in her head went on:

"You're looking for the fox-man...?" puzzled Kerissa.

The one with red hair who has gone to look for Hasan's mistress.

"You mean my father...?"

The vixen nodded.

You name him Gareth. If he finds your...mother...and I find him...then I will find Hasan again...with her...

She turned, and skittered away, retracing her path along the lane to the Boulevard.

Hasan was my *love. Look after our children. They will look after you as I have done.*

"Thelina...wait...!"

But the vixen was gone. When Kerissa faced back to the courtyard, the mad artist-god's work had become a whirlpool dwindling down ever smaller and smaller into its centre... funneling itself into the forms of three young foxes, who sat blinking in sunlight, their paws splayed upon the cobblestones, black button eyes fixed upon Kerissa...

"...Good morning, Miss Lloyd, is there anything I can do to be of service...?"

"...It's lovely to see you again, Miss Lloyd, now that things have quieted down some..."

The greetings continued as they made their way from the gates into the palace itself, encountering servants and officials, all showing a deference to Brandywine that puzzled Darya as they waited for her audience with the king.

"You were a lot more than just the second assistant t'the Royal Stationer, weren't you?" she asked.

Brandy looked away for a moment, shaking her head.

"Not really, Darya. I told you. It was just a promise I made to Queen Caroline...to help..."

"Robin knew better, just from talking t'Arabella..."

"Maybe tonight she'll feel more like being herself and you can get t'know her a little. She's had a really hard time of it in the last year, but I know she really really liked Robin. I think the reason she went off the way she did was because she hoped she would see him again…get t'know him better than the couple of days they spent in each other's company. She's such a sweet girl, my 'Bella. She hurts so badly whenever anyone else gets hurt…"

Darya whispered where Brandywine couldn't hear her…

"Just like you…"

They stood in an ante-room Brandy knew quite well, listening to the faint hum of voices on the other side of a closed door. After a few minutes, the voices ceased, and heavy footsteps sent a small tremor through the floor under their feet. The door opened, and a large mountain of a shadow stood framed there, Darya's royal summons in hand…

"Hello, Edmund," said Brandywine.

"Annie Branny!"

The mountain moved, embraced her and lifted her off her feet while Darya looked on in bewilderment.

"It's been…a few weeks…we didn't want to show up at a bad time…how's 'Bella…why're you here…who's this…?"

He put her down where her feet could touch the floor again and took a step backwards. Brandy pushed at him somewhere in the middle of his chest where she could get to him without working too hard. He grinned. Brandy sighed.

"Edmund, I think today is when we have t'come clean with 'Bella," she said quietly. "But the reason I'm here…" she went on, and turned to introduce her companion. "This is Robin's wife… Darya…"

Edmund began to ask an obvious question and then stopped, made some sort of face that was indicative of his awareness of the implications of the obvious, unspoken or otherwise. His gay welcome became a bit more subdued.

"Come in, please. We've gotten rid of the stuffy people. Ev's waiting for you."

He stood aside and ushered them into a room of slanting sunlight and a familiar face belonging to someone shuffling folders and papers away from the space on the table before him. Evrard looked up, smiled, called out a welcome to echo Edmund's own, before he rose and came round the table. He too embraced Brandywine, kissed her face and spent a very long time in the midst of one of her hugs, but his eyes never once left Darya...

"My lord..." began Brandywine.

"Don't...you...dare..." said Evrard.

With the same awful prescience as Edmund, he seemed to know exactly who it was she had brought before him.

"This is Darya," she said.

"Robin's wife," said Evrard.

Brandy nodded. Evrard turned away. Brandy turned back to Darya.

"Robin told you about Edmund and Evrard?" she asked.

The Bedford fisher-wife nodded.

"These two are the ones he spoke of," said Brandywine. "And maybe Edmund's brother Sebastian, as well..."

Andrew closed the door quietly behind him, stood awhiles as if staring past it, to where he'd left Arabella frowning at nothing, mulling over everything he'd said. At first he'd been terrified, expecting the worst, remembering how badly she had dealt with the horrors of the previous summer; but then it seemed as if something had fled away from the both of them, and when he looked at Arabella again, there was a calmness about her he'd not seen for a very long time.

"Thank you, Uncle Andrew." she'd said, leaning forward to hug him, and it was so much like once upon a time when he and her mother had sought each other for comfort's sake, that he simply let her hang on to him for as long as she cared to. Eventually she had let go, and he had been more than a little bit relieved to see the faintest of smiles on her face.

" 'Bella...?"

"It's all pretty crappy," she'd said, "but at least now I know. I'm not sure how I feel about any of it yet, but it makes sense now...finally. I'm gonna miss Zori so much... and I got so much t'make up to 'Rissa and Gareth..."

She'd started crying again, but there had been much less of despair in her tears, as if Knowledge had allowed her a renewal of the resolve and courage she had learned from her parents. Nicholas was waiting for him in the music room.

"Windy I think she's going t'be all right..."

Before either of them could say another word, there was a commotion downstairs at the front door. .

"...Why didn't you tell me? My Robin knew the king...?"

"He wasn't the king then, Darya."

"But now he is...and Edmund in his service?"

"For the summer...but if not for them and your Rob, an Antillian army would have come to the City on foot, and realised they'd been stranded here. It would've been dreadful.

I didn't say because I didn't want you t'be more nervous than you already were."

For a time, they walked along the Boulevard in silence. At length, Darya said:

"He's not at all what I expected. He doesn't act like a king."

Brandy agreed. "Not in any way you'd think, but he's learning. I knew that once he got comfortable with the thought himself, he'd get better at it. So far he's doing really well..."

Darya shook her head, looked at her and sighed.

"And you had nothing t'do with any of it, I'm sure."

Brandywine said, "*Almost* nothing. Are *you* gonna be okay?"

"I think so. If what the ki...Evrard...offered...is for real, it's a relief t'know we'll have a little bit extra every month. It'll make things a lot easier..."

"He doesn't make empty promises, Darya. It's never gonna make up for losing Robin, I know, but you'll never have t'worry about the children goin' hungry or not havin' a roof over their heads...and startin' yesterday, you'll always have a place t'stay here in the City."

"I have t'go back tomorrow, Brandy. Maybe you could visit...?"

"I think that would be wonderful, Darya. Every last one of us could descend upon your poor little town so you can meet the entire family all at once."

Darya smiled cautiously. "We should get back t'your house, Brandy. Your daughter's friend sounded really worried..."

"...Can I ask a favour of you?"

A SKULK OF FOXES

Edmund stopped in his tracks, halfway to the door.

"You're the bloody king, Ev," he grinned. "Why don't you just tell me what you want?"

"Don't be an ass. Between Annie Branny being all *My lord this* and *My lord that*...and your nonsense, I'm almost sorry I let her talk me into this whole thing."

"Quit moaning and groaning, it's not very king-like."

"Well *I'm* not very king-like, so there's no problem, is there?"

"What am I doing for you?"

"Go after Annie Branny and Darya Adair, let her know you'll be seeing her safe back t'Bedford. And then make sure you've got train passage for both of you for whenever she wants t'go home."

"So I'm going with her, just like that?"

"You're being an ass again, Edmund. I saw you looking at her. I think she'll appreciate your company..."

"And is there anything else, *my lord*?"

Evrard scowled at him, perched himself on the edge of the conference table and seemed to get lost in a sudden thought.

"In the end they're always the ones who have t'deal with the wreckage we make of the world," he mused softly. "They carry the weight of our lives and our stupidity on their shoulders, and sometimes spend *their* entire lives waiting for us to grow up into adults."

"You don't think she's too old for me?"

"How the devil should I know. Just go, all right? Stay as long you think you can get away with it, but get a horse for your trip back. I want you t'take your time...tour the Coastlands and the Westvales, let anyone you meet know that we're here

43

with whatever kind of relief or help they need, especially in Snowdon and that village my father burned t'the ground."

"I know what you're up to, Ev."

"Oh really...pray, overgrown person, tell me...what am I up to? And remember who you're talking to while you're at it."

"Of course, *my lord*. And good luck..."

"Good luck with what?"

"With whatever you're up to. I've decided it's not my place t'say..."

"...Is anybody home? Annie Branny? Uncle Nicky? 'Bella...?"

"Andrew and I are upstairs, 'Rissa. Are you all right?"

Kerissa's crown of bronze curls appeared between the balusters of the railing that ran along the edge of the stairwell. When the rest of her came along she stopped at the head of the stairs, and in response to the looks of surprise on the faces of her two "uncles", would have spread her hands as if to make something of a reply, if not for a small fox cradled in her arms, another draped over her shoulders and yet a third standing at her feet.

"I dunno," she said. "An hour ago I was in the middle of a major wiggins, but now..."

She shrugged, and scritched at the chin of the tiny vixen in her arms. The one around her shoulders licked her ear. The little dog-fox at her feet camped across one of them.

"They belong to Thelina."

Andrew asked, "Thelina...?"

"Hasan's honey...these are their babies..."

Nicholas said, 'Rissa, how d'you know that?"

A SKULK OF FOXES

"She told me just now...outside...she said she was gonna find him...and my mom and da..."

There were at least two questions that sprang to mind where Nicholas and Andrew were concerned, but Kerissa inched her way to a chair with the dog-fox clinging to an ankle, settled herself down, and proceeded to answer both of them without having been asked.

"My da's gone," she said, frowning. "He didn't come home last night. And I had this nightmare about Renard de Montenay..."

"Can we go back t'where Thelina *told you*...?" said Andrew. "Your *mother* talked with Hasan all the time, but all of a sudden it sounds like something *you're* doing..."

Kerissa shrugged again. "I guess so," she said. "I haven't really had the time t'give it much thought..."

" 'Rissa is that you?" came Arabella's voice from the hallway.

<hr />

Brandywine and Darya came through the front door of the coach house and heard laughter cascading down the stairs from the music room. Brandywine seemed to go pale with shock—the sound of squeaks and yips in-between laughter that was unmistakably the amusement of *two* young women—and then a look of joy and relief overspread her features as she turned to Darya.

"It's 'Rissa *and* 'Bella," she whispered. "Kerissa and Arabella... laughing...it's been so long I'd forgotten how t'even miss the sound..."

She grasped Darya's hand and led her up the stairway, until they arrived in the music room with their arms about each other's waists and stood silently waiting for someone to notice them.

Andrew and Nicholas stood with their backs to the stairhead, Kerissa and Arabella rolling around on the rug in the centre of the room with a trice of foxy kittens nipping and darting at them as they giggled themselves breathless. Brandywine made a sound that was halfway between a sob and a shout, clutched in Darya's arms, lost entire in watching her daughter at play with a smile on her face.

"Please promise you'll come visit me," said Darya quietly, and then they got noticed by everyone in the music room...

***

They undressed each other in candlelight, flickering shadows making some new mystery out of places both of them had known since they were children. This time however, there was an audience of three, all perched on the edge of Arabella's bed, six gleaming black eyes displaying a great deal of interest as more and more of them became less and less clothed.

'Rissa wriggled herself up against Arabella's front and whispered, "I wanna yummy you up till you ain't got no yummy left..."

The blonde girl made a happy sound and dipped her head down to where she could lick at the soft place where Kerissa's left arm met the rest of her.

"Okay...but you gotta go 'til I say stop, 'Rissa. I'm sorry I've been so weird. Right now all *I* wanna do is get yummy all over *you*."

"There's gonna be more bad stuff, 'Bella...I don't where my da's gone...and I had this dream..."

A SKULK OF FOXES

"I know, 'Rissa," she sighed. "We'll figure it out in the morning..."

Chapter Five – Another Tide Turning

"...'Rissa what day is it?"

"I dunno. Does it matter?

"Not really. I just feel like I've missed so many of them... Where's the foxes?"

Kerissa burrowed under their bedsheets and declined to answer, being quite certain that during the night she'd not quite managed to yummy up Arabella to where there wasn't no more yummy to be had. Early summer morning sunlight streamed through the bedroom windows, making dust motes dance in the air like foxlets materialising out of nowhere. Suddenly Kerissa had company.

"I found 'em," she said, though it was an hasty declaration at best, and in truth, not so much one of discovery as one to inform Arabella that *they* had been discovered instead. Eventually she was licked and nuzzled by foxy muzzles in enough places that her original intentions became secondary to not falling out of bed. Arabella rescued her. Three little fox faces popped up in a bunch of inappropriate places.

"I guess they really are Hasan's kittens," observed Kerissa. "Why don't you guys go see what's going on downstairs."

Instantaneously they were alone again.

A SKULK OF FOXES

"It would be spooky if it wasn't so cute," said Arabella. "They understand you..."

"It would appear so."

"Are they talking yet?"

"Any minute now, I suppose."

"Somethin's goin' on," drowsed the blonde girl. "I can hear voices all over the place downstairs."

'I don't wanna go anywhere right now,' said Kerissa, snuggling up to 'Bella's finer attributes. "This is nice. 'Bella are you okay?"

"I'm trying t'be, 'Rissa."

"You just tell me when it gets t'be too much all by yourself."

"I will."

"Promise me?"

"I promise...but we should see what's goin' on...'specially since... well...what you said last night..."

"I have t'tell you, 'Bella...but I'm still afraid—"

"Later is okay, baby. Let's go see what's up. I thought I heard the twins..."

───※───

They slipped into shorts and cotton jerseys, following the sound of voices down into the kitchen, where just about everyone they knew sat or stood round the long table, with Brandywine and Nicholas serving up coffee and tea along with fresh-baked bread, butter and jam, all the while dancing round three small foxes underfoot. Sebastian saw them first, rushed forward to stop dead in front of them, not sure what he should do next. Arabella kissed 'Rissa's hand from around her waist and jumped up to kiss his face.

MICHAEL SUMMERLEIGH

"I'm gonna be okay," she whispered into his ear, reached up her hands to his cheeks and kissed him again. "No matter what, I'm gonna try not t'leave you like the last time..."

He put his arms around her, shamelessly in tears.

"You missed Edmund and Darya," he said. "They left a few minutes ago. He's taking her back t'Bedford...gonna be gone most of the summer from the sound of it."

Arabella smiled ruefully.

"Well I got lots of stuff t'catch up on before then." Turning to her mother, she said, "I hope you got some toast and jam left for us..."

Brandywine nodded, looked at the crush of family in her kitchen and left off whatever it was she was doing.

"G'morning, baby."

"G'morning, mum...and it is...for now, anyway...the best..."

One by one, she got hugged and tearfully "welcomed", so much so that she turned to Kerissa and quietly remarked...

"It's like coming back from the dead."

...Before she waded into their midst and joined into what most resembled some crazy bit of early morning revelry. Kerissa trembled, looked up and found Nicholas watching her closely.

Eventually, everyone trooped upstairs to the front parlour, sprawled and laughed and went on as if loss and resurrection somehow had become a part of their normal everyday lives. Arabella cuddled with anyone who came near her, seemingly *hungry* for the touch of people whom she knew loved her and cared for her. The kits were everywhere, every bit as delighted with the attention paid to them as Brandy seemed to be with the smiles and laughter and newly-returned radiance of her daughter's face. Eventually, the party spilled into the courtyard...

"'Rissa...?"

She turned in the wake of everyone else, gratefully accepted Nicholas' arm around her shoulders, answered an unspoken question.

"I don't know," she said. "She seems t'be okay...last night I felt like we'd all finally come home t'where we could be peaceful again... but it's so sudden. I'm not unhappy about it, not at all, but...but...it's doesn't seem all *right*, if you know what I mean...? 'Bella would say it's wonky..."

Nicholas turned her round and enfolded her in his arms.

"At least she's back where we can help her."

Kerissa nodded against his chest.

"Meanwhile how are you? Branny told me you came running past her and Darya on the Boulevard yesterday morning; that you were really frightened...said your da was *gone*...? ...and you'd had a dream..."

They watched as outdoor furniture was liberated from the stable out back, Arabella soothed and stroked the chestnut mare she'd loaned to a dead man the previous year. The twins ran round shrieking as they chased fox-children all over the courtyard, and cats of all shapes, sizes and colours scattered before them, leapt for safety into the branches of the budding apple trees. Kerissa shivered.

"I'm scared," she said. "Da's not been the same since 'Bella came back, and now I don't know where he is. Last night I told 'Bella there was more bad stuff coming...so it wouldn't be a shock... and she said she knew. She said she knew and we could deal with it later... an' that was more frightening than anything else..."

"What about your dream, 'Rissa?"

"I already said, Uncle Windy. It was de Montenay, but after we'd left him for the crows. He was dead, but in the dream he was all falling apart dead, and he said he wasn't *finished* with me an' 'Bella yet."

They walked out into the courtyard, if for no other reason than not to attract attention to the pair of them head to head with each other, obviously involved in something a bit less cheery than the small celebration going on around them.

"What about your da? You said he didn't come home night before last..."

She nodded.

"I waited up forever until I couldn't stay awake, and then I had the dream and then I woke up and looked all over but he'd not come home at all. Those furry things showed up right here in your courtyard, and I ran away from them in the studio because I didn't know...but I think they were trying to...help...?"

Suddenly her halo of curls bobbed up from where Nicky had cradled her against his shoulder.

"What'd you say, Ysa?" she asked, at the trice of foxes who had appeared at their feet.

"Who's Ysa?" asked Jamie, who'd followed the foxes...

"She is," said Kerissa, wide-eyed, pointing to the vixen with a tiny white splotch in the middle of her chest. "And that's Yana, the baby, with Khalid their brother in the middle."

"This is a little bit weird, with Zori not here," said Thomas, who happened to be within earshot a few feet from them."

A SKULK OF FOXES

Diana, a step away from Thomas, shook her head from the middle of some invisible cobwebs, and called across to Brandywine.

"Branny is it too early for something stronger than coffee? I sense some serious shit about to happen..."

"What'd Ysa say?" asked Stella. She knelt beside her brother kneeling beside the little vixen and cupped the pointy face in her hands. "What'd you say, Ysa?"

Stella got her fingers licked for her trouble, but this time it was the wondering voice of Arabella who replied.

"She said Gareth has gone away..."

Like *déjà vu* all over again, they sat in the music room with large amounts of alcohol close by, and pondered over what almost all of them had managed to overhear or learn from being in the proximity of its source. Diana leaned forward from between Thomas' knees with a large balloon glass of cognac in one hand and a frown of concentration on her elfin features.

"It's starting again, isn't it?" she said.

"Something is...for sure," said Andrew.

"Are we gonna get sent somewhere else now?" inquired Jamie.

Nicholas shook his head, indicated he and his sister should sit beside him where they would be safe from exile. "You guys are almost grown up. You should stay..."

Alain seemed truly distraught for the first time in all the time they'd ever known him, his pale-featured face shadowed by doubt, evidenced by the way he kept Andrew close beside him.

"Gareth has disappeared?" he asked, looking first at Kerissa, then to the rest of those present.

"So it would seem..." said Brandy " ...And not in a good way, if disappearances are ever any good."

Arabella was the only one in the last hour who'd had nothing at all to say, letting herself be taken in tow by Kerissa and lying quietly with her head in her lap where they had settled down in the middle of the room; Sebastian had stretched out beside them, surrounding both of them in his arms, rocking them gently into what he hoped was a small cocoon of somewhere far away from the return of Reality

Kerissa said, "Before...before last winter...a vixen looked after me and Bella...twice... on the moors in the Carillon when we were being chased by Scandians...and then when we met up with Azim Sharad in the Westvales...

"She came to me yesterday...right outside in the courtyard...said her name was Thelina and she had been Hasan's mate...before he died...and then all of a sudden these three showed up..."

"Their children," said Nicholas.

Kerissa nodded and put her head down into Arabella's hair, where no one could see her face.

"We're the only ones who can find him," said the blonde girl. "We're the only ones can save him...maybe bring him back. Ysa said he'd gone away ...gone t'look for Zori... through one of the Thraxian Gates...but then somewhere else...wrong...*in-between*..."

Arabella's voice was frighteningly devoid of inflection...

"Does anyone know what any of this means?" demanded Diana, almost angrily. Thomas put a hand on her shoulder, leaned forward to kiss the cap of close-cropped dark hair on her head, and whisper something into her ear.

Nicholas clutched the twins closer to him. His face went from ghostly to a pale mask of unease, and he said:

"I do..."

WINDY'S STORY

"We've all heard a lot of this before...how once upon a time, our Gareth dreamt dreams of a place long gone from the face of the earth. Every once in a while, when we'd get into a bit too much of whatever it was we were drinking that night, he'd talk about them, how he'd wake up in a desert, not far from a deserted palace that seemed to echo with voices and something else...someone... calling to him..."

"That's when I met him," said Alain. "He'd fallen asleep on a bench near my shop and I recognised him by the colour of his hair...because Andy and Branny had described him t'me..."

Nicholas nodded. "It was in the midst of his dreaming that Kerissa's mother...our Zoraya...brought him to an ancient portrait on one of the walls of the dream palace...and somehow, through thousands of years, contrived to have him free her from her ancient prison by creating her image in a sculpture of stone.

"Suddenly, those of us so comfortably smug in the safety of our care of each other found ourselves under the spell of someone who had fallen beneath the magic of Gareth's own longing for a love of his own...and in bringing her into our time, brought also her infinite capacity for Love, and our salvation, though it proved to be twenty years in the making.

"Zoraya brought something special to what we had made for ourselves. With Gareth she made Kerissa, and with Kerissa, they gave my 'Bella the love of *her* life...but in the beginning I was not so much distrustful of her as I was curious, in the way any one of us would be curious about something more than just a sneeze beyond our ordinary...so I spent a great deal of time in the libraries of the City just t'satisfy my curiosity, and learned a lot more about things that I'd never even thought about thinking about in the first place..."

He paused, ran his hands through the hair of the mop-topped twins beside him, reached for his own glass of whisky and took his time while a small sip evapourated on his tongue.

"I never had much to go on," he continued. "Zori once mentioned she knew I'd gone *looking* for her in amongst all the dusty old books and manuscripts. Eventually I found a reference to her that, according to her own admission, was the *only* mention of her to be found anywhere...of her birth...her small accomplishments as a young woman...her sudden and mysterious disppearance from the world as we knew it then or now...

"But in the process of *looking for Zori*, I also learned about the history and traditions of the Magick into which she had grown, even as she had learned of her place amongst them herself. So to answer your question, Diana, it seems that *I* know something of what all of this is about...."

Forgotten for a time, three small foxes, who might have been anywhere until they decided to be somewhere, appeared at his feet. Brandywine came quietly from where she'd sat on the bench at his piano, came to sit beside him, gathering up the twins into her arms as she laid her head against his shoulder.

A SKULK OF FOXES

Nicholas...Nicky to his family...Windy to the family of his heart...continued:

"There was a man named Thraxus, who lived in Grecchia almost three thousand years ago, an Hellenic mystic and philosopher who was alternately hounded and praised for his beliefs, that managed to outrage those of his time as well as terrify them with its implications. Thraxus believed that we live in our own *continuum*... an ongoing sequence of Realities adjacent to thousands of ongoing Realities, sometimes so similar to each other as to be indistinguishable one from the next to most people who encounter them...and others that are so radically different from what we know, with elements that make themselves frighteningly apparent, and seem to exist only in our nightmares where, perhaps, we ourselves give them birth with the immensity of our own fear of the unknown.

"Thraxus postulated that there were *gates*—gates that led from one reality to the next...or simply just *another* version of our reality—that existed between them and the one we know. He said that there were thousands upon thousands of *us*, you and me, all existing at the same time, essentially in the same space, but separated from each other by the limitations of our own under-developed senses."

Diana knocked back a healthy swallow of cognac and rose to pour herself another.

"I'm sure that must've gone over just swell amongst the locals back then."

"In truth it didn't go over swell amongst most anybody just then," said Windy. "Thraxus was thought to have gone insane before he was stoned to death in the streets of Delos when he was not much older than I am."

"I guess you can't even try t'teach people stuff they don't wanna learn," observed Alain sadly. "True or not..."

"New ideas are what scare the daylights out of people," added Thomas, who'd spent too many years polemicising in service to his own unhappiness. "When Life gets difficult, we tend t'get stupid...fall back on stupid ideas that don't challenge our intelligence, but make us comfortable with the all the uncertainties of the lives we've chosen t'live...and they also give us targets ...people we can blame for our own failings."

Diana curled up beside him, dipped into her cognac before sharing it with a kiss. Windy reached for his whisky again, but then put it down, dragged Brandy and the twins closer.

"Well...Thraxus had lots of new ideas and they didn't go over at all well with the people he knew...but in our experience...and given the improbability of his ideas coming to us as a reality...through this bunch..." He nodded down at Ysa, Yana and Khalid. "What was a struggle for him—"

"Is an obvious Truth for us," said Arabella, sitting up abruptly. "Gareth has gone *between*...that's worse than just going through one of the gates. That's being somewhere no one should ever go..."

"..He was lured there...by something...someone...who led him into the dark...as payback..."

" 'Bella how can you be sure?"

She shrugged. "I'm pretty sure. I think I've been there."

"But payback? Revenge? We've been through that. You killed Azim Sharad."

A SKULK OF FOXES

"And I killed Renard de Montenay, too, but that didn't stop him from paying a visit to 'Rissa the other night."

She looked at Kerissa as if to say *I know you didn't tell me about your dream, but I know...same as I know what Ysa and Yana and Khalid are saying and can talk t'them just like you...*

She looked at everyone in the room in turn, and her green eyes sparked with tiny lightning flashes of gold that had never been there before Zoraya had brought her back.

"We should see if Gareth left anything behind for us," she said. "Something that can tell us where t'begin...how t'find the gates..."

Brandywine appeared dazed, listening to someone who looked like her daughter and, up until less than an hour before, had seemed to be Arabella finally back to a place where she could start living again without guilt or fear. Now she felt as though her daughter had become not so much a stranger, as just someone gone utterly strange.

" 'Rissa and Sebastian should go back t'the studio and look..."

"What're you gonna do, 'Bella?"

"I'm gonna try t'remember...everything...from when I was gone."

❦

They all agreed to return to the coach house that evening, to plot a course of action. Sebastian and Kerissa went off to Old Princes Street. Tom and Diana followed them, Alain and Andrew and the twins all went home themselves, leaving Nicholas and Brandywine with Arabella and the fox kittens.

"I didn't mean t'frighten you," she said. "All of a sudden I had these things jump into my head, and then they just came out as words." She turned to the foxes, who stopped their playing and stood still, as if listening. Then they flickered away into the afternoon sun.

"I told them they should go with 'Rissa and Sebastian," she smiled. "T'make sure they were safe. I'm gonna go lie down for a little bit."

She wandered upstairs. Her parents sat together, saying nothing for the longest while. Nicholas watched his daughter as she left the room, padded down the hallway...listened until he heard the door to her bedroom close behind her. At length, he said:

"I wonder if maybe we've been through some of these gates before."

"The day Zori took us to that palace floating on the ocean," said Brandy.

Nicholas nodded. "I think so. I'm sure Zoraya knew all about them, so it's certainly not impossible. Did I ever tell you where *I* went that day?"

"You never did, and I never said where I'd gone. I ended up in the place where I was born, Windy. I saw my real mom and dad. They were very sick. My father brought me here t'the City because they couldn't take care of me anymore."

"I can't imagine giving you up for anything short of something like that," he said, stroking her hair. She closed her eyes and made purring noises.

"Where did *you* go, Windy?"

"You said I just pitched myself off the Promenade and into the bay for no particular reason, but for me, I was leaning into the pool in the courtyard of that palace and I fell in. I saw Robertson, Branny. I saw him, and I saw a lovely young woman with him whom I'm sure was Rochelle de Montenay, because all he did was smile and say *I found her*...just as he said he would... I can't help feeling there's a connection; that *we* have some knowledge worth knowing, even though we don't know just what it is yet."

"Windy d'you think maybe Robertson...with his painting...the one he began the night the City sang...d'you think he somehow opened one of these gates, and then went through?"

"I think that's exactly what happened, Branny...and somehow you were the one gave him the key...that bit of advice on how to make the shadows work, with a little bit of this and a little bit of that added to his palette of colours...and the City waking up in the process..."

"I'm gonna have t'think about that for a while...."

"Maybe it's part of what we need t'know, is all I'm saying..."

Arabella closed the door of her bedroom behind her, put her back to it and closed her eyes, letting tears fall from them and down her face as they chose. In the afternoon, light was never so bright here as in the morning, so when she blinked her eyes open again, the gold lightning sparks had gone softer and the shadows in the corner of her room had grown deeper. She put her head down and cried soundlessly, went to her closet and reached inside for her sword-belt, leaving the pistols behind because she knew they wouldn't work on the other side, and her bow because...

MICHAEL SUMMERLEIGH

"I guess it doesn't really matter what I wear or bring t'the party," she said to no one.

She felt her lips growing cold...and all the memories of all the days when she had been just ...Arabella...now drifting away...lost again in the imperative of saving the ones who loved her.

Her breath became ragged; her eyes blazed and grew dim.

"I'm coming..." she whispered, and flickered away into the Otherwhere.

"...Sleeping...she's sleeping...we've not seen her since everyone left just after lunchtime..."

"Annie Branny she's not sleeping...she's not in her room..."

Kerissa was frantic. They had gone back to the studio on Old Princes Street, found a small collection of books her father had gotten from the libraries of the City, and then, with the appearance of Hasan's children, had known at once what was in the wind.

"She's gone..." said Kerissa. "I can't believe I was so stupid t'believe she would be all right with this."

Nicholas strove to keep incomprehension from turning him useless. He recognised all of the books Sebastian and 'Rissa had brought back with them, had consulted them himself half a lifetime ago. He looked up from where he'd strewn them across the top of his piano and struggled for composure as he spoke to their family, come together again as planned.

"She's gone after Gareth. We thought she'd come to terms with what Zori had done, but once she found out what really

A SKULK OF FOXES

happened, and that Gareth had gone, I think she knew all along what she would do..."

Alain and Andrew and the twins were speechless. Thomas stood in a corner of the music room with his head down, trying not to snarl with frustration, the knowledge of his own helplessness, the absence of any choice he himself could make that would help. Diana seemed to be only one there with any semblance of calm, her arms around Brandywine and her face set into a cold resolve to go anywhere and do anything...if only someone could tell her where to go or what to do...

"We have t'find a way t'go after her!" cried Kerissa, squirming from Sebastian's arms. "We can't just sit here. We can't just let her go off on her own all over again t'save us, without lifting a hand to help her!"

Windy turned, caught her as she fled wildly into the middle of the room. They met there, and in a heartbeat were mantled in a shroud of three rust-red yearlings guised as foxes.

"We have t'go..." said Kerissa, and then they were gone.

Part Two

THE THRAXIAN GATES

Chapter Six – The House in St John's Mews

"...Sebastian...Tommy...do something!" cried Diana.

"Like what, Mom?"

"I dunno...something...anything..."

She refused to let go of Brandywine, whose face had gone blank with surprise and then suddenly filled with a look of complete bewilderment...

"Where did 'Rissa and Uncle Windy go?" asked Jamie. There was a note of terror in his voice, and Stella reached for him instinctively

...As Brandy rose up from Diana's arms and went to them, now with a quiet resolve across her features and a fierce light of determination in her green eyes.

"They've gone t'get 'Bella and Uncle Gareth," she said quietly.

"But where have they gone, Branny?" asked Stella plaintively.

Brandywine smiled. "It doesn't matter, honey," she said. "Wherever it is they've gone is where they'll find Arabella and Gareth and bring them home."

"Not like last time please," whispered the little girl.

"No, Stella, not at all like the last time...I promise..." she said, hugging them both.

She looked up and beckoned to Alain with a glance, moving them to the stairs, making it plain it was about time for any kind of distraction for the twins. When they were gone, she turned to everyone else in the room, met their questioning gazes and confusion with a frightening calmness.

"Please don't feel like you have t'go...I hope you'll all stay you know this place belongs to all of us...but I need a little while t'think...by myself..."

Andrew took her by the shoulders, looked her in the eyes.

"Of course we'll stay, Branny...but you call if you need us...okay...?"

She nodded, leaned forward to kiss his face and turned away, walking slowly down the hallway to the rear of the coach house, seeking refuge in the bedroom she shared with Windy. She went to her dressing table, and there opened a small envelope containing the mailed response to a wire she'd sent to the Carillon just over a week ago, to Windy's parents, informing them cryptically that "...Arabella has come back to us..."

Written in Alexandra Wyndham's elegant hand was a brief note:

!?!?!?!?!
We shall be there within a fortnight...
Alex

"Please come soon," she whispered, and folded the note-paper back into its envelope. Then she went to the bed and curled herself there, her back against the tall carved wooden frame, with her arms wrapped her knees.

A SKULK OF FOXES

"...We should send word to Edmund, he can come back as soon as he's delivered the Adair woman to Bedford."

"He's got other business as well, Mom. He told me last night—Evrard sent him off with some project or another. He said he'd likely be gone most of the summer."

Diana growled. "The brat doesn't have t'be so damned kingly all of a sudden. We need Edmund here—"

"No we don't, Di..." said Thomas softly. "Edmund is fine where he is, for the summer or however long it takes him t'do whatever it was Evrard needed him t'do. We'll find a way t'deal with this ourselves..."

"Tommy don't try t'—"

Beverley crossed the music room in three strides that rattled the glassware on the sideboard, and lifted her almost bodily from where she sat.

"You can trust me with this, Diana," he said. "We know just about everything about all the things that've brought us t'this moment, but we've really had very little t'do with the actual workings of any of it. Let's let things unfold now and we'll all deal with whatever happens together, okay?"

She looked at him in amazement for a moment, and then nodded, once.

"Okay," she said. "But I'm gonna need more brandy...or something..."

Thomas grinned. "*That* we can manage," he said; setting her down again. He re-crossed the room and poured cognac for her, looking over his shoulder at Andrew and his younger son. Sebastian nodded; Andrew took a glass of claret. After having delivered both, he went back to sit beside Diana.

MICHAEL SUMMERLEIGH

"...So now we'll wait a wee bit, maybe overdo the alcohol if we get bored, and see what happens..." he said quietly.

Andrew knocked on the door, heard a whispered response before he opened it and went to sit beside her with a deep concern in his dark eyes, reaching for her without even thinking.

"I thought I had t'go t'the bathroom," he said, smiling cautiously.

"Sure y'did," replied Brandy. "How'd you know...?"

"You're my best friend, Branny...my oldest friend. Actually, you're the first person to ever really *be* my friend."

"You never told that."

"Well it's true, but after a while it wasn't important...not t'me, anyway. Once it happened it never seemed like I had t'put it into words...it just felt right, like it had always been that way."

"Me too, Andy. Cosy up with me like we used to...I miss Windy so much already..."

"You've got the best hugs, y'know. I told Alain right off he'd have t'practise a lot if he ever wanted t'measure up..."

"I guess he's done okay, then. It's been a long time."

"I lied t'him, Branny. He was great from the very first day...not quite like yours, but—"

"Just like Alain."

Andrew nodded. "Are you okay?"

"I'm working on that, Andy. I was scared t'death at first, but then I realised that Windy was with 'Rissa and those little magic foxes...and wherever they'd gone 'Bella was probably close by...so I'm not so crazy with the wiggins anymore, but

A SKULK OF FOXES

I have this feeling I should know what I should do next and that's what I'm all about now....trying t'figure out what it is. Right now I think the most important thing we can do is make sure Jamie and Stella don't get too frightened by all of this. When 'Bella died I thought they'd never stop crying..."

They spent a bit of time as they'd spent it so often in the days when they'd first met, and then she sent him off below stairs to look after Alain and the twins. When he was gone, the door closed quietly behind him, she put her arms around her knees again and pondered upon whatever it was she was supposed to do next.

Maybe if I just sit still and be real quiet I can find out... she thought hopefully.

"...Alain's really scared," whispered Jamie, looking at Alain's back as he made hot chocolate on the stove.

"So'm I," said Stella.

Jamie nodded. They were at the far end of the long clerestory table that filled half the stone floor of the Wyndham kitchen, suddenly finding in themselves a bit of *controlled* terror, as if instinctively they knew that not falling prey to the wiggins was a good thing for all concerned. He took her hand.

" 'Bella makes it sound funny." she said.

"Makes *what* sound funny?" demanded Jamie.

"Havin' *the wiggins*," giggled Stella. "It doesn't *sound* at all like anything we should be worried about."

"Don't be silly, Stel," admonished Jamie. "It's serious. How come when Uncle Windy and 'Rissa disappeared everybody got them?"

"You mean the wiggins?"
"Yeah...how come...?"
He listened to himself and grinned at her.
"Maybe you're right."
Alain showed up with hot chocolate in three big mugs.
"You guys doin' okay?" he asked cautiously.
Jamie and Stella nodded nonchalantly and asked if there were any of those small marshmallow things to go with...

"...Your father is making me crazy," she said to Sebastian. "Sitting here doing nothing is...is...well I'd kill for another cognac but then I'd have credibility issues."

Sebastian stifled laughter.

"Mom, you gotta realise that we're all on pretty shaky ground here."

"Sebastian...dammit...don't make light of this. It's serious...!"

"Well of course it is...but what're we supposed t'do? Dad was right about us never really bein' in on the wonky stuff—"

"*Wonky stuff?*"

"Hey I'm just going with the girls on that."

Diana looked woefully at the dregs of her cognac and sighed.

"I hate not being able to do *anything*."

"Nothing is all we *can* do right now, Mum," looking at her glass. "Y'know...I could use another one of those myself. Afterwards...for now...let's just follow Dad's lead...?"

Chapter Seven – Arabella in Witchlight

She opened her eyes, closed them again, quickly, dizzy with the rush of Memory that flooded into her consciousness. She recognised the brief sensation of being afloat on an invisible tide; the sudden sense of being wrenched loose from everything and everyone she had ever known. It had been no more than an instant in her experience, though in fact six months had passed before Zoraya had been well enough to search her out, leaving the relative safety of the lands beyond the gates behind, sacrificing herself to find her. But in that moment, that single breath of Time where she had existed on the edge of... *something*... she had gone the length and breadth of whatever it was she had come to, seen every dark cobweb in every corner, seen Light hammering its way into Darkness, Darkness swallowing Light; had watched lifetimes unfold before her and then fold back upon themselves. The images and emotions had never come back to her in any recognisable *conscious* memory, but now she knew...now she was *aware*...and while the imperative driving her was not one of hysterical urgency, it was, nevertheless, undeniable and inexorable.

There was, too, a physical sense attendant upon her presence in this place, different from that of her first *visit*. Then there had been confusion and fear, a total loss of self...the sensation of no sensation at all with regard to the flesh and bone and muscle of her body. Now she vibrated within an almost delicious drowsiness, as if having wandered too close to the lands of the Dead in the past served to heighten that which she risked by her close proximity to them now. She realised she was burning with a feverish intensity, yearning to simply give in, close her eyes and relinquish all thought and duty in blind worship of what she had called *the Big Yummy*...when she and Kerissa became so lost in each other that nothing else in the world mattered. She sobbed aloud, and heard the sound swallowed up by Silence...forced herself to open her eyes again.

"Arabella..." whispered a voice in her head, and she looked down to where a dog-fox stood at her feet.

"Hasan...?"

The fox nodded.

Why are you here?

"Gareth is gone."

I know this.

"Is Zori close by?"

Hasan shook his head

She has gone to look for him...in Qaraq-al-Ossa...*the Bone Castle...*

"That's why I'm here."

You should not *be here. You have been and gone before. More than once is not a good thing.*

Arabella shrugged, knelt beside him, reached for him and saw her hand pass through an image of Hasan fading away before her eyes.

"Don't go...!" she cried.

Go back, Arabella.

A SKULK OF FOXES

"I don't know how..."

Go back...

"Oh sure...it's something I do on a regular basis..."

She stood again, took stock of her thorough lack of preparation—shorts and a jersey and a sword-belt.

"I'm ready for just about nothing this way," she murmured to herself. "I wish Hasan would come back...or maybe I'd not gone t'so much trouble t'be here by myself. 'Rissa would know what t'do..."

But she thought that 'Rissa would have had even less chance of surviving here on her own, and hoped no one was following her. She looked around, trying to get a clear picture of her immediate surroundings, and the funny peculiar way everything seemed to have such a hard time just *being*...

No big surprise that Thraxus guy went 'round the bend she said to herself. *He was probably on t'something with his gates and whatnot, but I wish he'd taken the time to write a guidebook...a few maps...a couple of good places t'stay the night ohmygosh 'Rissa I could use some yummies right now big-time.*

What surprised her about wherever it was she had arrived was how bland it all seemed... harmlessly full of rocks and trees and sky and earth that seemed to beg for something to distinguish them one from the other; that the gate she had gone through had led to a place that was little more just a pale reflection of something she might have left behind, rather than something in and of itself.

"It's not got anything *intrinsic*," she observed, feeling a vague sense of smugness at finding a word she'd never used before.

MICHAEL SUMMERLEIGH

"That's because this place is on the border, close to the end of all things," rasped a voice beside her. "Just like you..."

She whirled, her sword out in an arc of dull silver that went through the body of the creature beside her as if it were nothing at all, a robed figure with a hyaena smile and a dagger-hilt tucked neatly up beneath its chin.

"I have not forgotten you," said Azim Sharad, as he melted into the earth.

For the longest time in her life, Arabella had never truly been frightened. When she was young, the luxury of being owned by Kerissa, surrounded by a family who adored her, had insulated her from even the possibility of it intruding into her awareness; but when Fear finally found her, came knock-knock-knocking on the door of her life, she had always responded with an outrage of sorts, that it should dare, and though it was never a conscious thought, she knew that her greatest defense against being afraid was that outrage, the simple instinctive reaction to fight back like hell. If someone had ever suggested it was something had been gifted upon her by her mother, she might have laughed...but only for as long as it took her to realise it was an absolute truth...

The place she had come to was nowhere near *in-between*. She knew that...she knew it was...simply...somewhere...on the other side of one of the gates, one other version of the life she'd lost and regained...and instinctively she looked round for anything that could provide her with a sense of where she might be in relation to whatever else was there...

A SKULK OF FOXES

When that failed to happen, when the landscape around became chill with its own lack of *intrinsicality*, too far from the normal reality of the young woman stranded there, she *did* become frightened, but only so long as it took her to remember why she had come in the first place.

She looked at the empty space where Azim Sharad had been, and said:

"You *better* remember me. I killed you once and I can do it again. Stay clear of me and the people I love, or somehow I'll make good and sure you can't exist anywhere ever again."

She looked at her sword-blade, and wondered how it seemed to bear no resemblance to the weapon she'd taken from her closet. Another pair of daggers on her belt appeared to mirror that lack, and a little fox-voice whispered in her head that she had come to place of shadows, as if in that moment it was all the explanation necessary. Arabella smiled. She looked into the sky of the Otherwhere and saw the reflection of the moon voyaging across a shadow sky, where clouds shone black against the wan pale light of the night, and stars were tiny scratches there that led into darkness.

"I'm gonna find you, Gareth, wherever you are..." she promised, and knelt with a flint and grey almost-steel from the pouch on her belt, scrabbled about at her bare feet for anything that might welcome the warmth of a small flame. She managed the smallest of fires, a pale flicker of light in the suffocating emptiness; then she stood sword and daggers upright in the ground and went a few paces away, to where she could see their shadows in the firelight...their *reality* in the wasteland she had come to.

MICHAEL SUMMERLEIGH

"Now you've got trouble," she said, drawing them up from where they lay on the ground.

She began to wander...aimlessly it seemed...because there was nothing about where she was beyond this particular gate of the madman named Thraxus to give her a sense of where she should go to remedy the situations that had brought her there in the first place, though one thought did come to mind...

Hasan said Zori was looking for Gareth in the Bone Castle...

Chapter Eight – Nicholas in the Borderlands

Ysa told him *Is not really the place we wanted to be, this...*

Nicholas agreed wholeheartedly, though not in any way he'd yet managed to adequately convey to a pair of less-than-year-old vixens scampering around his feet in the middle of a place that looked like it hadn't seen an inch of rainfall in the better part of two thousand years. The little one...Yana...seemed distracted...

"Where's 'Rissa gone off to?" he asked.

Stay here do not move said Ysa, and disappeared...

Yana camped at his feet, pointed her little face in a dozen different directions at once, obviously a bit less focused than her older sibling.

"D'you speak?" he asked.

Of course...

"Where are we?"

Somewhere...

"That's not very helpful. I need to find my daughter, the girl my daughter loves, and her father..."

Am the littlest one, me. No one tells...

"It's not funny."

Not being funny, me. Ysa will know...having patience, you...

MICHAEL SUMMERLEIGH

Nicholas fought against the natural reaction his daughter called *the wiggins*, surveying the immense and total wasteland of the place he had come to, that was, in its own sterile way, so totally familiar as to be frightening any time he tried to place it just where and how he'd ever been anywhere near it. And then it became startlingly obvious.

"These are the Emerald Gardens!" he whispered.

Not the same Yana whispered back.

"But almost," said Windy.

Yes... said the little girl-fox.

"So where are we?"

Not knowing, me...on the other side of a gate...very old, this...older than the flower...but is bad...

"You know this for a fact?" he asked.

Ysa has said. Khalid came once, but ran away...said was a very bad place...

"But it's the Emerald Gardens sort of. There's the lake and the place where the concerts are held....the bridle paths that go off—"

Not the same...

"Your name is Yana?"

Is...

"Yana, d'you know where I can find 'Bella or Gareth or Kerissa?"

Ysa maybe will know...

She huddled against his trouser leg and he could feel her trembling. Bad place or not, he scooped her up into his arms and strode out from under the shelter of a rock outcropping, began a descent to what *he* recognised as what might have been the man-made lake in the recreational park of the City, if the

A SKULK OF FOXES

Antillian fleet had perhaps not made a wasteland of it a few generations earlier.

He crabbed his way down a hillside that was devoid of any living thing he could discern, his eyes drawn to a pair of structures that seemed to float in the distance—a pavilion of sorts on the far side of the lake, and something palatial that seemed endlessly miles away, but risen up into an ashen sky wherein floated two glaucous suns that gave no light of any value to anything living.

Ysa said to wait.

"She'll find us, Yana," Nicholas said soothingly. "I want a closer look at the lake…"

The little vixen crawled up around his shoulders as they descended into the valley, the hillside disintegrating under his feet with every step, threatening to pitch them both downward onto a steepening slope of razour-sharp scree that would have shredded both of them bloody in seconds. Yana whimpered into his ear.

Bad…very bad…must be careful, we…

"Why is this place so bad, Yana?"

Khalid and Ysa say someone is here who is never dying…

Nicholas considered that as he tried to negotiate the slope beneath them…the implication of it in the greater context of his own experience with Death, and the inference most likely to be drawn by someone in his position.

"Well then…" he murmured aloud, "perhaps we *should* have waited for Ysa…:"

He heard Yana make a small foxy chuckle.

Am funny, you…

Nicholas grinned and forgot to pay attention. His right foot slid through a mass of much-less-than-solid stone, twisted one way while he and Yana went the other. He landed on his back, the vixen clutching madly round his neck as they slid downward almost to the foot of the hillside before he managed to find some purchase with his left foot. He could feel blood seeping through the tattered linen of his shirt, found himself nose-to-nose with his companion, two dark-eyed pools of foxyness conveying a large sense of I-told-you-so...

Is big ouch, yes?

He nodded. "Pretty much," he said ruefully. "Hang on, sweetheart, I've gotta get back on my feet..."

He sat up creakily, already feeling blood drying and linen clinging to his back. He caught Yana up in his arms and lunged forward onto his feet, hopping the last few yards of their descent until he found balance on the level ground below and began a slow lurching progress toward the edge of the lake. He sensed rather than truly felt the little fox's nervousness, but found her naturally grinning face staring up at him.

Loving these 'Bellas and 'Rissas, you...

"And my Brandywine, more than the world," he whispered back to her. He felt her nodding against his chest.

Is the same for the one who is my mother...loving Hasan...

"He was always very mysterious...but he and Zoraya were new to the rest of us. We didn't know then what we know now."

Not being afraid, you...Thelina says we are for looking out for you...are having magicks, we...am waiting for them, mine, because I am the small one...

Nicholas found a damp little black nose pressed up against his face, drew breath and fought against a small bout of blurry in front of his eyes. They lurched onward, towards a lake that only *just* resembled one he knew well, and in the strange sickly light of two suns, yet seemed dead and lifeless, an empty black slate of what might not have been water at all, still and unmoving as they approached....

...And yet still seemed to give off the foul odour of something not long dead, though he knew of nothing that could possibly have found life there within recent memory. As they came to edge of the lake, what small amount of light from the twin deaths of sunlight overhead grew dim and cast them into twilight. Nicholas looked up and saw a massive shadow winging its way across the leprous sky. He stumbled again, reached instinctively for support and found the skeleton of a tree in his grasp, falling sideways heard it snap with his weight before he managed to swing it round to keep him and Yana from pitching face-first into the waste. Yana whispered:

Is coming, him...

"Who, Yana?"

The one who did not die...the king...

Nicholas struggled upright and saw a monstrous ragged flutter of sickening yellow tatters arrow towards them and float over the surface of the lake, moments away, a hooded face unseen in amongst its shadows. He heard a shriek of outrage echoing across the water that still would not move even a ripple in response to the passage of what came at them...reared up above them upon the marge of the dead water scarce a handful of paces from them. Nicholas clutched the splintered bole of the tree, struggled for balance that he might lift it up in their defense...and felt the onrush of the apparition come to a dismayed halt...felt the hiss of rage that flooded over them in a charnel stench.

"Give it me," demanded the yellow king.

Nicholas shook his head.

"Not for our lives," he said, raising the splintered length before him. "Come any closer and you'll have it in no way of your own choosing."

The creature howled, the tide of its anger rolling over them like the breath of a plague.

"You will be made to pay."

Nicholas retched onto the sterile waste at his feet, spat bile from his mouth and grinned.

"Not by you," he said. "I'll end you here and now unless you tell me what I want t'know."

The creature snarled with unseen lips

"Begone. I have known your kind...ages ago...when they stole what was mine...the flower..."

Yana whimpered in his ear. Nicholas stood himself up as tall as he could and laughed...

"What you've lost means nothing to me. I've come for people I love. Where do I find them?"

He heard the creature smile, the rattle of Death in its throat.

"Welcome to the borderlands of Caracosh...where we will surely meet again in Qaraq-al-Ossa. The Bone Castle waits endlessly and you will come to me in your own time... with my blessing..."

Nicholas shook his head.

"No blessings from you, my friend. This place...this *place* dies endlessly... and you are dying with it..."

A SKULK OF FOXES

The creature snarled without making a sound. Nicholas reached up with his free hand to where Yana clung to his neck, and put his fingers in her ruff.

"You can't touch us here...*or* where I come from," he whispered. "I think perhaps you were tamed lifetimes ago..."

And then there was silence...and yellow tatters in the light of dying suns drifting away on no breeze at all.

Chapter Nine - Kerissa Goes to Ground

She sprawled in tall grass in what might have been sunlight...on a hillside looking down over a sheltered vale watered by a stream that made no sound as it slipped silently past a thatched cottage only a score of paces from its banks. She felt a brush of warmth against a bare thigh and found a young dog-fox beside her in the grass.

"Khalid?" she asked.

The dog-fox nodded.

"Where are we?"

Khalid shrugged. *Gone from everyone else...*

"That's not very helpful."

Khalid shrugged again.

Not knowing...only we are where we have come to...

"Have you ever been here?"

Being very small. Thinking to have been new here...safe...

"Thelina gave birth to you and Ysa and Yana here."

Khalid nodded.

A secret place...

"Not *tha*t secret, Khalid. *Someone* built this cottage...and look...goats and sheep and chickens in the yard... "

The fox agreed whole-heartedly, and shrugged again to indicate he had little else of any value to add to their

A SKULK OF FOXES

conversation. The goats and sheep and chickens milled about the yard soundlessly.

"We're not anywhere near where we need t'be, are we?"

Not knowing this, the fox apologised. *Things happen as they want to...*

"I'm not certain I know what that means, Khalid."

Not of this place, we...must wait for happenings to see what to do.

"Can you explain that a bit better maybe?"

Khalid shook his head. Kerissa struggled to her feet, somewhat dismayed to find that as had been the case in a nasty dream not so far distant from what passed as her present, she had come to a place somewhat beyond her ken without benefit of clothing.

"Well...how lovely..." she thought aloud, and started down the hillside. "Maybe there's something t'wear in the cottage...and if not...well...I read a book once where the heroine seemed t'manage okay in her altogether..."

As she came nearer, the cottage door opened. The shadow of a flock of birds overhead fell across an ashen-faced young blonde woman who slipped to the ground...slowly... clutching her belly, eyes wide and green, but glazed with pain as they tried to focus on something behind Kerissa and her foxy companion. The young woman soundlessly called for someone named *Jacob* before she fell sideways beside the door. 'Rissa rushed forward...horrified...puzzled...

"Bella...?"

...And felt a rush of something run *through* her...a young man...barefoot and shirtless... frantic...his passage like a small whirlwind that twisted 'Rissa round, sprawled her beside the garth-yard gate and then down into a yawning emptiness that was lined with flickering images racing past the arc of her descent like some lunatic kaleidoscope. She grew dizzy, and then felt she might be sick until she felt Khalid's presence beside her... heard the reassurance of his "voice" in her head...

Not being afraid, you...

She nodded and closed her eyes, haunted by the despair she had seen in her lover's eyes...

When she opened hers again she was back in a place she *did* recognise—the endless expanse of the Carillon moors in starlight, echoing with the distorted battle-cries of armoured Scandians closing in on a pair of travelers, one of whom looked unsettlingly like a mirror image of herself, whirling round to try to somehow shield the blonde woman from the cottage who lay at her feet.

"'Bella wake up!"

She howled in frustration, dropped to her knees, and looked curiously down to where a feathered arrow had torn into the artery in her left thigh, raining blood blackened by moonlight down over the prostrate form beside her...

"'Bella wake up...please wake *up*!"

...Listening to the *thunk* of another arrow shredding into her chest...going cross-eyed with...surprise...to see 'Bella's eyes staring up at her...calmly...

"Go...go now, Kerissa. I'm not Arabella. You can't save me or Nicholas or your father by staying here."

She felt a small muzzle close gently round an upflung hand and drag her away into somewhere else...

A SKULK OF FOXES

A total darkness...coolth...a whispering of sound not unlike something she had encountered not so long ago...

A faint humming seemed to enfold her body...envelop her like a second skin... creeping into every pore to vibrate against her bones.

She recalled two arrows but felt no pain...thought her eyes must be open, but with the absence of light could not be certain...tried to call out to Arabella but felt that whatever sounds she was making were being swallowed up in the insistent humming.

Remembering Khalid she "called" to him...felt/heard him answer her...

Am here with you...
Where are we?
In the earth...
Buried?!?!

Blind panic suddenly gave way to a tingling in a place where her fingertips might be, as if they had gone to sleep and then to pins-and-needles...re-awakening with a spark...the merest hint of not-darkness.

She focused all of herself on that spark and watched it grow until she was quite certain she recognised it as a pale blue-white effulgence.

It was a word/thought she had never used before, yet she knew it for what it was and became aware of its source on the forefinger of her left hand...a soft warming radiance come from a moonstone set in silver...

She realised that the entirety of her body was cocoon-ed in earth; that any kind of movement should have been impossible; that she was, in fact...buried...and yet still alive...somehow breathing in something that should have left her gasping for breath and choking to death before she became a bloated thing of rotting flesh...gone from the world...gone from those she had come to save...gone...just gone...from everything and everyone...

Am here with you, Kerissa Davies...

Khalid, how can this be...?

She felt his foxy shrug, the one he used when he had no answers, yet remained unfazed by whatever had raised the unanswerable question in the first place. She felt his calmness, and what passed for his reply:

. Am your mother's daughter, you...

If her eyes had in fact been open to see the suffocating reality/weight of her tomb, she closed them now, but felt the growing light/breath of her mother's moonstone filling her body to merge with the humming of the earth around her because now she recognised it...the voice of the City...the earth...on the day when her mother and Nicholas had raised it up to save them all from the Antillian armada...

Must go now, me, Kerissa Davies...not worrying, you...back soon......

She felt his sudden absence from her awareness of him, fought another momentary bout of panic, but heard his "words" again...

Am your mother's daughter, you...

Chapter Ten – Brandywine Takes a Stand

Occasionally one of them would leave for an hour so, taking turns to look after the necessaries of their own lives so Brandywine would never lack for as much company as they could provide in any given moment. Alain left to make sure the warehouse and market stalls were running smoothly; when he returned, Sebastian hared off to the Amaranth Palace to inform Evrard of the latest *developments*; upon his return, Diana went off to teach an afternoon class in her studio. Thomas maintained the all-round sense of calm whilst keeping up a steady relationship with the Wyndham wine cellar, and Andrew basically kept an eye on Brandy, the twins, and things in general.

The afternoon was wearing on towards dinnertime when the cobblestones in the courtyard began to echo with the arrival of a horse-drawn carriage. The twins rushed to the music-room windows and announced the arrival of *Grampa Fred and Grammy Alex,* then raced down the upper hallway to tell Annie Branny while Andrew went downstairs to welcome them...

"...Brandy didn't say you were coming," he said, shaking hands and accepting hugs.

Alexandra Wyndham kissed him.

MICHAEL SUMMERLEIGH

"I sent a note a few days ago, Andrew, in response to Brandy's wire that said Arabella *had come back*...?"

Andrew nodded. Alexandra looked at her husband and the pair of them looked mystified together.

"Andrew how it that possible?" asked Nicholas' father. "'Bella died...six...seven months ago...whenever it was, she *died*, Andrew. How on earth did she just *come back*...?"

Andrew drew a deep breath and begged for a small amount of time to answer the question.

It was a measure of the closeness they all had come to know that neither of them made any kind of protest, only had the carriage emptied of their traveling bags and, with Thomas and Sebastian to shuffle them up into one of the upstairs guest-rooms, followed Andrew into the ground-floor parlour where he poured whisky for Frederick and wine for Alexandra.

"There's an awful lot of explaining we need t'do," he said. "Things we never got round t'mentioning back when they'd just happened. It wasn't so much they needed t'be kept secret anymore...just that once the reasons for the secrets were gone, it didn't seem all that important that anyone needed t'know the whys and whatnots. You were here for some of it," he concluded, looking at Alexandra, "but I don't think we ever quite got round t'telling the whole story..."

Frederick Wyndham looked mildly put out over his whisky, but his wife just nodded and asked if everyone was all right.

"Well...I guess the answer to that is kind of no answer at all, Alexandra. How 'Bella just *came back* is a long one all by itself. What's going on now is like a bad postscript to that, though we're all trying t'keep from getting crazy over it."

A SKULK OF FOXES

Their looks of total bewilderment were somewhat lessened with the distraction of Jamie and Stella's arrival from upstairs.

"Branny's comin'...!" they announced in their usual fashion, loudly, and together in the same breath, at the same time launching themselves into the arms of their grandparents-by-proxy.

They heard Brandywine's soft footfalls on the stairs, turning to her as she crossed the front hallway and came into the parlour...stopped short when she saw Nicky's parents and started to cry.

"You came...thank you so much..."

Alexandra said, "Brandy is it really true...Arabella is here...?"

Andrew said, "Well she was...but now not so much because of the postscript thing I was talking about. Unfortunately, Nicholas and Kerissa have gone off after her..."

"Unfortunately," said Frederick Wyndham.

Andrew made a rueful face and nodded. "It could change, but for right now we're going with 'unfortunately.'" When he turned to Brandy, she was looking at him like he'd lost his mind. He grinned cautiously.

"I'm just tryin t'be optimistic," he said. "C'mon, kids...let Grams and Grampa breathe a little bit."

When they had the parlour to themselves, Alexandra turned to Brandywine.

"Whatever s going on, it's going to be all right?"

"I don't really know, Mum," she said. "I think I figured out what I have t'do, but it's gonna take a little bit of time. We just have t'hope it's not gonna be *too* much time...for Windy, 'Bella, 'Rissa *and* Gareth."

"Gareth is gone, too? We should sit down for this, shouldn't we?" said Frederick.

Brandy nodded, and spent the better part of the next hour trying to make what had become commonplace to *les Boulevardiers* sound reasonable to them, rather than the ravings of someone gone thoroughly mad.

"Well I wondered how the Findhorn suddenly decided to tear the daylights out of the City *and* turn the Antillian ships into scrap," said Frederick, shaking his head. He stood and poured another whisky for himself and wine for Alexandra. "But you say there was a flower...it was...a *magical* flower?...and Zoraya knew all about it...?"

Brandy nodded. "And a fox, too. I know it sounds crazy..."

"Honey, if anybody else was telling us this story..."

"I know, I know..." she said.

"And Zoraya is gone, as well?" asked Alexandra.

"She is, Mum. She used the flower t'get Arabella back, but the only way she could do it was to trade herself and the flower for 'Bella...and it was more than Gareth could bear... losing her... even though he knew what she was gonna do...even though he knew she was doing it so 'Rissa could have Arabella...but she left a note for 'Rissa...said she'd never done anything like it before...that there could be...

"Repercussions?"

"Yes ...repercussions...consequences...and now it seems like Renard de Montenay and...the thing that started all our troubles....because Zori did that last magick...it let them back into our lives even though 'Bella killed both of them..."

Alexandra put her wine glass down on a side table and went to sit beside Brandywine, taking her by the shoulders.

A SKULK OF FOXES

"Branny you're not going to...to...go after them yourself...?"

"I don't know how t'do that, Mum, and even if I managed it I wouldn't know what t'do once I got t'wherever they are" she said, "but before everybody disappeared, me and Nicky talked about something that happened a long time ago, and it seemed like maybe there was something I *could* do... t'help get them all back safe."

Frederick Wyndham had come to stand beside them.

"I'm not going t'pretend I have any real understanding about any of this," he said quietly, "but I know for a fact that whatever you and Nicky know t'be the truth of what's going on is enough for me...and for Alexandra...

"We're here for as long as it takes...whatever whatever it is takes to be taken care of..."

"We'll get them back," said his wife.

"Yes we will," said Brandywine. "I wanna make all of this stop once and for all..."

Chapter Eleven – Arabella in the Otherwhere I

She walked silently, cautiously with each step, because Silence seemed to be that which existed most comfortably in the place to which she'd come. For the most part her progress was through an empty reflection of what might once have been elsewhere, in a place inhabited by real people with real hopes and real dreams and some inkling of what might come to pass in a real future. The place through which she walked now held none of that promise, no promise at all, for better or for worse. To Arabella, in the only way she could describe it, it most resembled a *lifescape* painted by someone who had never lived. When she came to a hillside overlooking the standing stones, saw the hundreds of souls marching blindly into oblivion for lack of anywhere else to go in the place they had come to share, she stopped and dropped her shadow-sword, wept shadow-tears for the end of Hope...

"We could be so much more than this," she said quietly

She listened to herself, and wondered where the thought had come from.

"It shouldn't be so hard..."

Death is always close by...a breath away whispered Hasan. *You think too much...your kind...and you say you are better than us for all the thoughts that come into your heads... but you suffer*

A SKULK OF FOXES

under the weight of the things you know...and always want more, not recognising you already have enough...

She looked down at her feet and found him grinning up at her.

"That's not funny...at all..." she said.

Hasan's face moved sideways, and for a moment she felt what it might be like to shed foxy tears.

No...it's not funny at all, Arabella...

"But how do we live...how do we stop from being afraid...?"

By living...only that...

"Hasan, you gave yourself for her."

What else could I do? I was only a thought in the lifetime of the universe...but my thought was long enough for you to give your kind a promise of tomorrow. The thing that took you would have taken everything...everyone... given enough Time...now it is worse...

"Hasan I miss her so much... 'Rissa never says...Zori was my second mom, she was—"

My mistress...and she knew from the beginning, Arabella Wyndham...long before the stars ever dreamt of you or your family. The life Gareth gave back to her was given so that you and Kerissa would have each other, and the world another chance to become what it was meant to be...

"Hasan..."

There is no room for your sadness in this place, Arabella. There is only the Bone Castle before you, and winning a place for Gareth and my mistress...together...

She fell to her knees beside him, and this time, when she reached for him, there was a warmth and a ripple of his fur beneath her fingers.

MICHAEL SUMMERLEIGH

And there is no room for me anywhere but with her...
"Hasan, how do we get through this? Why do we do it...?"
There was one last fading foxy smile.
You *call them* yummies. *Goodbye, beautiful girl...*
When she looked up nothing had changed. The greyness still went on forever. The endless parade of souls below her went on and on and on into the endless horizon of endless struggle and the ever-present promise of disaster. Her own question rose up to challenge her.

*How...*why *do we do this...?*

The thought of *yummies* shared with 'Rissa suddenly became infinitely more than the thought of simple playfulness that it had been a moment before. She couldn't describe it in words, yet it was perfectly understood, all the answer she required.

"It *can't* be that simple," she said, but she knew that it was true; that for all the blessings of her freedom, the *gift* of never having been cold or hungry or alone, safe in the love of her family, it truly was that simple if only everyone else could have that chance, the *awareness*, to find it out for themselves.

She climbed to her feet, shaking her head at the absurdity of going to war for Love... barefoot in a pair of shorts and a cotton jersey with a double-daggered swordbelt of shadows around her waist. Once upon a time her father had said to her:

"Sometimes we have t'bloody our hands in order t'stop them from bloodying our lives."

It had only just managed to make sense to her then...but it made perfect sense to her now, though the doing of it was become no easier.

A SKULK OF FOXES

"It's your job, Arabella," she told herself aloud, where no one could hear her. "You just be quiet now and do your job."

It became problematical within moments. She felt the ground beneath her feet begin to tremble, but somehow everything aboveground began to tremble with it...as if the landscape metaphor she had thought of a few minutes earlier was become in fact some sort of three-dimensional canvas being shaken by an unseen hand. As the trembling of the earth increased in intensity she found it more and more difficult to stay on her feet; then the air was filled with an enormous *creaking*, and the standing stones below her...the horde of mindless pilgrims approaching them...all seemed to blur in and out of focus, and the air began to crack, fissures radiating outward as though a pane of glass containing the image of the standing stones and its parade of doomed souls was shattering before her eyes... and was being replaced by another immediately behind it, that was *almost* an exact copy of the original image.

The difference became apparent as she re-lived the nightmare she had experienced the previous summer with Kerissa at her side. Again those who trudged silently towards the stones turned to face her, but now the eyes that had been dull and empty with no real active intelligence behind them were filled with despair...rage...and a virulent hate. They turned on her in a perfect synchronicity—as she'd seen arrows of migratory birds change direction in mid-flight—and climbed toward her in an utter silence far more terrifying than any kind of sound they might have made. Arabella realised she had just witnessed the disintegration of whatever it was that separated two different realities...understood she was...once again...in a mortal danger...picked up her sword and drew a dagger to meet them.

Another difference became apparent to her; that those who now climbed the hillside to reach her were not the same souls as before; that these were the casualties of the horrific conflagration that had consumed the town of Trowbridge and its inhabitants. The eyes that blazed upwards at her were framed in charred skeletal faces skimmed with burned flesh and ribbons of hair; with every movement of the legs beneath them, tatters of blackened flesh fell away from bone and scattered into the air like the cinders of the inferno that had claimed them in the blind vengeance of the ancient sorcerer she had known as Azim Sharad. Arabella whimpered something that might have been a prayer... *Please not again*...and swung at the first of the nightmares to reach her.

Her blade severed its head from the rest of its body. A dagger thrust splintered through another's ribcage, and up into a shriveled heart beating time to the terror in her own. She began to scream as she flailed at them, scything them down as she wept, with tears that rained sparks of gold from her eyes, that met with the tortured remains of townspeople she had never known and slowly dimmed the ferocity of their hatred and damnation, smoothed their ruined features into attitudes of something that might have been gratitude as they sank down and disappeared into the earth.

As the entire population of Trowbridge came at her, she ceased to have any cognisance of Time or Self. She became a saviour and final executioner with every stroke of her sword of shadows, every thrust of the shadow-dagger in her right hand. Now the obscenity of eyes fastened upon her softened into supplication, and the carnage she wrought became an almost religious act of redemption for those she slaughtered—a final dealing of Death in the name of Peace. On her knees again, she wept for them all, watered their remains with her tears and saved them from their own fear.

When next she looked up she was alone. The standing stones, as before, were gone, and the stand of shadow-trees behind her, on the crest of the hill, sheltered the immensity of a night-black draft horse who might have been known as Diomede in some other more kind semblance of Reality. Arabella sheathed her sword and dagger, loosed his halter from a low-hanging bough and climbed up onto his back...

Chapter Twelve - Nicholas Crosses the Border

Yana was shivering uncontrollably, gripped in terror. Nicholas scooped her from round his neck, whispered meaningless sounds meant to soothe her fright, cradled her against his chest until her trembling ceased.

Said was bad, me...very bad...

"I know," replied Nicholas, "but we did okay...and now we have an invitation to exactly where we wanna go..."

He could feel Yana shaking her head against his chest, heard a small sigh.

Crazy, you...

Nicholas found it difficult to disagree.

"Sometimes it's the only way you can get by..."

Am hoping finding my magicks soon, me...

Nicholas smiled down at her, ruffled his fingers down her back and listened to a foxy equivalent of purring.

"Me too," he said. "You could be right about the *crazy* thing...and that means we'll be needing some help."

Not afraid, you...?

"Only of not being able to get my girls and Gareth back home safely."

He looked left and right for the shortest route round the lake, thinking a quick look into the pavilion on the far shore

A SKULK OF FOXES

would be worthwhile, perhaps a place where they might find some further indication of what awaited them in Qaraq-al-Ossa, wherever it might be. Their progress was slow at best, Nicholas favouring his injured ankle, but it became evident to him quite quickly that this progress had very little to do with the amount of effort required to make it; that they might arrive at the pavillion in a matter of a few footsteps, or spend an endless what-passed-for-day-in-this-place to get there at all. He put his head down and struggled along, heard Yana making small optimistic song-sounds against him that seemed to merge with something coming from the pavilion itself...

He recognised those *sounds* as orchestral music, vaguely familiar, as if the few notes that came to him from across the lake were part of a suite or symphony he might have heard before. He stopped for a moment, put his head to one side and strained to hear the distant scoring of horns and strings... puzzled...and of a sudden, uneasy to know exactly what he was listening to. When he raised his head up the pavilion lay directly before him and Yana, a vast covered space surrounded on three sides by an ascending amphitheatre of ranked benches full with elegantly-dressed patrons in the throes of outrage.

"Do you see what you've done?" came a voice from beside him.

"I don't understand," said Nicholas to the robed figure at his side. He reached for Yana on his shoulder and found her gone. "I've done nothing...certainly not here..."

The robed figure, a tall slender man of great facial beauty, stood stiffly and smiled down at him with teeth filed to points.

"You disclaim *Tristesse*?" he demanded. "You deny that you are the composer of this symphonic abomination?"

"I know you," said Nicholas, breathing heavily as he leant on his staff.

"And I know you...very well... *You* are the father of the trollop who consigned me to this place...and now the one who shall be responsible for the end of these innocent people by their own hands...drowned and buried beneath the weight of the bitter thing you created in the wake of her death."

A taloned hand disengaged itself from the folds of his robe and made a sweeping arc to encompass an audience gone mad, tearing at each other's finery and their own throats, inflicting murderous wounds in a frenzied carnival of despair.

"I wrote *Tristesse* over twenty years ago!"

"Not this *Tristesse*. This one you made scarcely six months ago, to make the world pay for having lost your precious cunt of a daughter."

"I never wrote this! Not one note of it did I ever put to paper!"

Azim Sharad smiled a second time, and shrugged as if to say *What an insignificant detail*...as the earth of the pale twilight landscape grew dark with rivers of blood rushing toward the stage that was sheltered by the pavilion.

"Enjoy your stay," he sneered, and undid the collar of his robe. From where its hilt was buried beneath his jaw, he drew forth a poniard that steamed and sizzled in the half-light. "Perhaps you will return this to the slut who gave it to me."

The point came at Nicholas' chest in a blur of motion that was swept aside by the brush of a vixen's tail so that it came to rest instead in the body of the staff in his hand...and slowly dissolved down along its length. The sorcerer hissed and reeled backwards as if struck by the staff itself, his impossibly elegant

A SKULK OF FOXES

face for an instant become the mask of something half-human, fanged and dripping with hatred, before the figure itself sank into the ground. Nicholas looked at the place where it had disappeared, found two vixens looking up at him.

Next time waiting, you said Ysa.

Looking quite pleased with herself, Yana licked carelessly at her tail where it had flicked aside the knife-thrust of the sorcerer.

Next time waiting... she said, echoing her sister. Nicholas nodded to both of them.

"Next time waiting," he agreed.

He looked back to the carnage resulting from the symphonic expression of grief he had never written, and found there was no one in an amphitheatre that did not even exist. The pavilion itself was empty of any life, littered only with the corpses of leaves and the fossilised skeletons of tiny insects with the misfortune to have expired on the paved expanse beneath the roof of the enclosure. They crunched underfoot, swirled around the paws of his four-footed companions. Nicholas looked out over an expanse of nothing he recognised, save perhaps the faint outline of a castle on an horizon lifetimes away. He felt incomparably weary, and could have wept for wanting his old life back, with two little girls playing at his feet, and Brandy with her arms around him.

"Please help me end this quickly," he whispered. "Time must be important to save Gareth. Why can we not just hang on to teach other and go where we need to be? 'Rissa told us how they came to be in Bedford when my daughter killed the sorcerer..."

'Rissa did this. We are too young said Ysa *With you we cannot do this yet...*

"Then Hasan...Thelina...?"

Our mother is not magick...and if our father could do this thing...if he would *do it...still it would not be good...*

Nicholas sagged against the outer rail on one side of the pavilion, wordlessly begging for an answer.

There is a balance that we must be keeping. We all of us must be where we are meant to be if we ware to be winning our lives from those who have new life from bringing Arabella back from the dead...

"How d'you know that?"

Am the daughters of our father and our mother, we said Yana. *But* a*ll magick in this way works...*

Ysa nodded up at him. *Is Truth-speaking, my sister. The fox-man has no one to tell him this. He goes blindly in search of his lost love, not knowing, lost in his grief...*

Nicholas closed his eyes, his thoughts frantic in four different directions. He recognised an unreasoning panic in himself, struggled to master it so the questions that might quell it could find some way to be asked

"What happened here?" he cried. "With Azim Sharad? You saved me from the dagger, Yana...but then it...melted...?"

Your stick grinned the youngest of the two.

Did our grandmother never say the story of the flower?

Nicholas thought back over almost a year and nodded wordlessly.

A SKULK OF FOXES

It is the tree by the lake, Nicholas...in the place that no one living has been in more than a hundred lifetimes...upon which once grew the one flower...

Nicholas closed his eyes again, thinking furiously...processing... sorting this new wonder from the maelstrom of recent events, and striving to place it within the context of all the other things that had come to visit the lives of his family.

At length, he asked "Will we be able t'get there in time?"

Two fox faces looked first at each other and then shrugged up at him.

Am hoping so, we... said Yana

Chapter Thirteen - Kerissa in the Underworld

She had very little in the way of anything sensible to support the feeling that she was moving at all. The sensation/terror of being buried alive slipped away somewhere behind her and she could not say when it had happened, only that movement had become effortless, her forward motion lit with the light of her mother's ring. The earth enfolding her teemed with wriggling shadows and she could hear the rustlings and scurryings of the small creatures who made their homes, often lived their entire lives there...suddenly could smell and taste the rich warm damp seethe of Life becoming real around her, striving upward into the Light and downward into the Dark...all the same...each one a thread in the cosmic tapestry.

I wonder how 'Bella knew... she mused to herself...*How she could possibly know what I dreamt...* even as the answer came to her. *My mom could do that...part of her is in 'Bella now...*

The thought was comforting, though it made her heart ache with longing for 'Bella's touch, her hands on her body, the dreamlike sense of them lying together, flying together, and then the release, the sense of silly stupid happiness that someday might become so commonplace as to be unremarkable, if only the world would leave them to live out their days together.

A SKULK OF FOXES

She whispered *I love you 'Bella* in a very earthlike voice that rippled through her surroundings, vibrated through the fabric of her new reality, and found that the light of her moonstone had widened to flood through a greater darkness than the one that had snugged round her.

Now she stood in a vast undeground cavern, with the vault of its ceiling so far above her that it became lost beyond the reach of her moonstone's light. Here again she became acquainted with *effulgence*, everything around her softly alive with an inner glow that made evident the complete utter strangeness of what might easily have been an upland meadow...aboveground...but for the muted colours and the not-quite-*rightness* of the place itself.

She laughed *gorse and heather* to herself, remembering a night on the Carillon moors, and a burr caught in Arabella's knickers before they found shelter, and a vixen named Thelina come to rouse them from the path of an errant band of Scandian invaders.

"You should've waited for me, 'Bella," she said. "I know why you didn't, but we're no good without each other. I worry about you all the time, and I still have no idea where I am, where I'm going, or what I should be doing t'get my da back to us..."

We must find Qaraq-al-Ossa said Khalid. *Ysa says your mother is to be there, and Arabella must go there too so the fox-man can be saved.*

"D'you know how t'find this place, Khalid?"

Once am being there. Is bad very bad place, so ran away, me...maybe can find it again...

"We have to find it."

MICHAEL SUMMERLEIGH

Knowing this...but is bad place...dead things not dead...and the Bone Castle where is your father to be looking for your mother.

Kerissa thought a question.

No...only the dead can go through and come back...

"Then why, Khalid...what good can we do...?"

The sun girl is dead. She may go through...

"'Bella... ? 'Bella's not dead, my mom brought her back... "

Has been, she...

Kerissa shivered. Arabella most assuredly *had* been dead. The miraculous thing her mother had done had been conveniently forgotten in the few weeks of having her beloved *dead* Arabella back, warm in their bed...

"Khalid, you're givin' me the wiggins..."

Am sorry, me came a foxy shrug. *Is only the truth...*

Kerissa nodded, and the vast cavernous space expanded around her, the semblance of upland meadow growing barren as it sloped gently down to the meander of a jet-black river so wide that it filled half the space to the horizon now before her.

Khalid said *Our way into the Death-land, this...*

Kerissa had read the mythology of the man who had postulated gates and alternities... recognised the river, though skeptically, since it had been, up until that very moment, only mythology. In consequence, when they had traversed the meadow, she was not surprised to find the ferryman waiting for her—a broken thing half has naked as herself in mouldering rags that once might have been clothing.

"Passage to the other side, m'lady?" inquired the ferryman with great unctuosity. He bowed deeply before her, eyeing Khalid with wariness from beneath his lowered brows, but only for a moment before his eyes grew bright with interest for

A SKULK OF FOXES

Kerissa's own lack of clothing...the glow of her skin and eyes and the tangled promise of shelter between her thighs.

"Perhaps the young lady cannot buy her way with common currency. Perhaps she would trade favour for her way across the flood?"

Kerissa shook her head at such presumption, though in fact there was in her the pressing question of just how she and Khalid might cross the river *without* the participation of the troll. The ferryman caught the wink of light on her left hand, and seemed perplexed at seeing it on her forefinger.

"You have crossed before," he said.

Kerissa said, "Never."

"Yet I know you...and that ring on your left hand. I have seen *that* before, and not so long ago..."

"Perhaps only the shadow of it, certainly not the shadow or reality of me."

"Nevertheless..."

"Nevertheless nothing, my friend," said Kerissa. "My companion and I need t'get across this river...or whatever it is..."

"Then you are mad. No one comes here willingly."

Kerissa shrugged. "It's just necessary. My little friend is pretty certain the place we're looking for lies beyond your miserable little province."

"There is nothing beyond here, my lady. Only the Land of the Dead."

Kerissa smiled. "And the Bone Castle...Qaraq-al-Ossa..." she said, and scoured him with light from the moonstone on her hand.

The ferryman fell from drooling and obsequious hunger to his knees.

"My pardon, lady..." he breathed into the sterile earth beneath him. "I have mistaken you for someone else."

"Only for someone who *might* have gone before," she replied. "And all of a sudden I don't think I really need any help from you at all..."

"M'lady—"

"You can keep your place here, for whoever comes after me...but just now I think you'd best stand aside, so I can be on my way..."

She waved her hand across the earth where it met with the still water, and a blue-white light etched a narrow path across the flood, one side to the next. She scooped Khalid up into her arms and went past the ferryman, stepped onto the way she had crafted from need, and did not look back.

"My mum's come this way," she whispered to the little dog-fox. "We're going in the right direction..."

Chapter Fourteen – Arabella in the Otherwhere II

Everything went out of focus as the draft horse wheeled and turned to plunge down the far side of the hill, which suddenly became bathed in cold sunlight. Arabella could see her breath streaming out in front of her face, but felt nothing of the cold. She and the horse stood on a headland of the far north, watching villagers below fleeing inland from the ice-strewn shore, deafened by the scream of projectiles tearing through the frost-ridden air of the ocean to rip their village to shreds behind them. She saw one villager on horseback break away from those on foot, outpacing their progress into the hills above the fjord before disappearing into a break in them as he rode eastward. She kicked her heels against her own horse's flanks and again they turned, down off the headland on a course roughly parallel to the horseman below.

As they came again to level ground farther inland, Arabella looked to her left, scanning northward in search of the lone rider, but found instead another shivering of the air around her, and beyond it...herself...matching her own eastward progress. She shook her head at imaginary cobwebs and tore at the halter in her hands, urging the horse to move into the shimmer between them, felt the cobwebs become real as they passed from their reality into the one beside it. Time and distance telescoped in upon themselves as the northern steppes shifted, shuddered, and became the rolling hills of the Carillon moors, and she now racing well to the south of her quarry as the course of his flight intersected with that of a band of armed Scandians on foot. She saw his horse swerve away from them, gain perhaps a hundred yards before the horse stumbled, and fell to the ground with a chance arrow in its lungs. The rider leapt from his saddle, landing at a dead run with the shouts of the Scandians filling the air in his wake. Arabella leaned forward, clapped her heels a second time, and added her voice to those of the invaders, hoping the man on foot would hear her, alter his course to meet up with hers that much sooner...

Her horse thundered down through the near-frozen surface of a small stream and churned its way up the northern bank in time for her to see another Scandian arrow take the fugitive to his knees before the moors disappeared in front of her and she could almost feel Time slowing to a crawl as Scandian arrows at close range tore Kerissa from a wagon-bed and sent her flying backwards. Arabella turned, screaming her name, and Sylvain de Montenay smiled at her from his place on the wagon bench with the gaping wound in his throat.

"We don't need her around, do we?" he asked pleasantly, though there was a distinct and unsettling gurgle in his voice. "Not just yet, at any rate. I want some time to play with you first..."

She leapt from the wagon bed, tumbling down through the briars and loose gravel flanking the bed of the railway line running parallel to the Findhorn on its way to Elysee. Kerissa said:

" I can't live without you, 'Bella."

A SKULK OF FOXES

"I won't go anywhere, baby, I promise, please don't die," she said, pushing at the place between 'Rissa's breasts where the arrow leaked blood over her fingers.

"It's too late, 'Bella. You're too late."

"No, 'Rissa please no..."

Somewhere someone laughed derisively, and Arabella felt like she'd been plunged into a whirlpool sucking her down to the bottom of the ocean...quiet...dark...the swirl and the rush all fading away as she loosed the halter of a mountainous black draft horse from a low-hanging tree branch and climbed up onto his back...turned him round and headed eastward, looking for a place where she could be in time to save Trowbridge from the thing they called Azim Sharad.

<hr />

After a while she said "I'm getting tired of this," out loud, because there wasn't enough sound in the place she was in now. "Wandering around looking for this Bone Castle in a place I've never even heard of..."

The meadows and hills of the Westvales were not at all unpleasant as the black horse alternately galloped and cantered their way through them. The sky overhead wasn't quite the comfortable cornflower blue she would have preferred, the sun as warm as she would have liked, or the birdsong quite as cheery on air that felt like it had gone a bit stale, but all of it *was* recognisable.

"Something funny's going on," she mused. "Funny peculiar, like maybe I'm playing tricks on myself...like maybe these different realities are just mirrors of the stuff in my own head instead of being *real* all by themselves... "

She let that thought wander around in her mind on its own for a while, trying to sort out where all of her recent experiences began and ended...what could have been waking nightmare or a conjuration set upon her.

"...So maybe they *are* real all by themselves, but then...how likely would it be for me t'be bouncing around all over the place into realities that are more like mean little gifts of all the things that scare me the most?"

This thought seemed to strengthen the one before it; that Thraxus had been more correct than not in his hypotheses about the gates; that they *did* in fact exist in and of themselves, with shivery bits of something between them that got thinned out so if you were aware enough, you *could* move from one reality to another...

...And that meant her experiences were a departure from the normal (whatever *that* was)...not nearly random enough to be credible...and *that* meant it was likely that some*one* or some*thing* was manipulating them to confuse her...keep her from the one alternate reality she sought as she stumbled from manipulation into a Thraxian reality and then back into another nightmare of her own creation.

"So all the wonkiness is coming from...the de Montenays...?"

She shook her head. Renard de Montenay and his son never had shown any capacity to do damage anywhere but in their own world.

"Chakidze then...being cranky because he knows he can't do me any real harm...but then I have t'explain how that happened, and if he can't really hurt me, then it's *almost* logical

A SKULK OF FOXES

somebody or something else has t'be in this game and I have t'figure that out too..."

All of which brought her to one last question and realisation.

"When me and 'Rissa saved her mom it happened because Hasan...and 'Rissa too, I suppose, being Zori's daughter...zoomed us from the City to Bedford...through a gate...in a heartbeat. And his kittens can do the same sort of thing...but I've never been able t'do any of that stuff before, yet here I am in the middle of it all, travelling all by myself...

"...Because now I'm just as much Zori's daughter as 'Rissa's ever been...maybe even more because I was dead, and she traded her life t'give me back mine. Gareth's in trouble because of me. Bringing me back brought everything back...sort of...but I still don't know what I have t'do t'fix anything, except t'stop letting Chakidze...Azim Sharad...*someone*...keep me running in circles..."

And as that thought ran through her head, the Westvales started to shimmer and shatter and fall apart around her.

Chapter Fifteen – Nicholas on the Rocky Road to Wherever

The first time Nicholas turned around to see what kind of progress they'd made, the pavilion was no longer in sight. Ysa and Yana had trotted on a few more paces, but now came back to stand at his feet, tails twitching and amusement registering on their pointy faces.

Khalid says nothing works right here said the elder.

"I've been noticing that," said Nicholas in return, "and before we met up with the dead sorcerer-musician guy, I could have sworn there was a castle on the horizon... but now there's nothing...just more of this lovely landscape."

He looked around distastefully, at tenuous bits of growth struggling up through the barren excuse for soil. From far away on his right hand, the sound of what might have been thunder reached their ears, and in that direction Nicholas noticed smudges of dense cloud in the empty sky, and a faint glow rising up along the horizon as if someone had ignited a huge bonfire.

"I suppose it explains why we're not meeting up with anyone but the local hobgoblins and whatever they feel like conjuring up for our amusement. Nobody in their right mind would come here unless they had nowhere else t'go."

A SKULK OF FOXES

The vixens seemed to nod in agreement, and then started off again in the direction that Nicholas thought to have seen the castle. It was slow going at best, his ankle becoming more and more painful with every step; when he stopped to squirm out of his boot and examine it, the entire joint had already begun to swell and purple up his leg and down into his foot. Yana came to lick at it cautiously...then Ysa. Both stood back as if waiting for something to happen, then took a step away with an obvious show of frustration and impatience. Yana wagged her head forlornly and looked up at him.

Still not making magicks, we...and ouch is bigger now, yes?

Nicholas patted her head gently in commiseration.

"It's all right, Yana," he said. "We've just got t'do the best we can for now. Be patient, you, and eventually everything will come right."

He grinned at using her pattern of "speech", and failed to notice Ysa staring down at his ankle...intently...looking away as if weighing some course of action not to be shared, before she lashed one forepaw across the top of his foot and laid it open to the small bones beneath the skin. Nicholas sat bolt upright in agony, wide-eyed as blood poured into the ground under his foot and small flowers sprang up through the crimson pools gathering there, runneled off to make more of them, bright spots of yellow, violet and white, writhing their way up into the dull grey light. He looked at Ysa in amazement, could not open his mouth to ask *Why?* through the pain, only to clench his teeth as lightning tore through his leg and he fell backwards, eyes now closed...*betrayed?*... knowing that now he would never reach Qaraq-al-Ossa...never come to Gareth's rescue...or anyone else's for that matter...

And then it was gone...the unimaginable pain not even a memory...

He lifted his head up and stared down the length of his body to where both foxes had dragged his long splinter of a walking stick and plunged one end of it into the mangled flesh Ysa had made with her claws...watched them drag it away and the ragged flesh knit itself together, stemming the tide of his blood, and then, slowly, turn the bruised and swollen flesh back into what it had been before his fall on the hillside.

Better now said Ysa. She nipped at a violet flower and chewed slowly, keeping her eyes fixed upon Nicholas' face. He looked at his foot, and at her.

Yana thought if we could not fix you then the tree might have magick for us...

Nicholas slipped back into his boot, stood and bounced lightly on the foot.

"Time t'be on our way then," he said, and trembled...

What they encountered on their *way* was not anything any of them would care to remember ever again. Their progress became a constant struggle to deal with every nightmare Nicholas had ever experienced, every fear that had ever crossed into his mind to disturb the halcyonic passage of his days as a privileged and favoured child to an adult with no concerns for his future well-being. He recognised the weight of it...again...as he had recognised it a score of years earlier, written it into a symphony, and almost been buried beneath its weight had it not been for the people he had kept from falling to their knees,

A SKULK OF FOXES

and a sorceress come into their lives to save his home and his family and bring his daughter back to him.

Nicholas lived and relived every horror he had ever imagined as a child, railed and wept with every step as the vixens led him onward into the heart of the land called Caracosh, where it seemed to him that he began to move in a whirlwind that never stopped rushing round and past him, drawing breath from his lungs and Hope from his heart. In the quiet places where his love and creativity lived, he recognised the irrationality of every moment, that his secret terrors should in no way to be able to mount such a sustained and unrelenting attack against his piece of mind, yet he suffered in despite of that awareness, and the onslaught upon his emotions was debilitating every bit as much as it was a cause for pointless anger.

There was no recognisable day or night in Caracosh. It was an endless rebuke to positive struggle and rest, inexorable and cruel in its ability to crawl into his darkest and deepest doubts about everything, whether or not he'd ever actually encountered any reason to doubt any of it. It was mindless. It was the Soul of the Universe, the Chaos against which one single human soul could never prevail. Nicholas had two vulpine souls to save him from despair. When he fell exhausted upon their way, they crept into his arms and sang him foxy songs of Hope and Redemption; when he fell into nightmare sleep in the endless grey day, they crept into his dreams and sang some more.

When he awoke they would stare up at him anxiously, to see if they had lost him. Nicholas would get to his feet, lean upon his splintered staff and look up at the featureless sky...find himself in yet another corner of his old life...

...Standing in late morning...waiting...at the end of a cobbled courtyard—known locally as St John's Mews—rimmed with the last tatters of winter snow, that cowered up the stone walls enclosing it and against the trunks of apple trees just beginning to bud in the early spring sun. At length the solicitor arrived and they exchanged greetings, shook hands as he apologised for being somewhat later than than the time they had agreed upon the previous day. He fumbled in his coat pocket for keys, found the proper one for the door to the converted coach house, stepped aside as it swung open into a short tiled foyer.

"It's not been available until quite recently," he said. "Likely it will lease rather quickly."

"What's with all the cats?" asked Nicholas, having noticed them in amongst all the branches of the apple trees, and scattering in every direction when he surprised them with his presence...

The solicitor shrugged.

"They seem to like it here."

Nicholas said nothing, only walked past the entryway until it opened to his left onto a front parlour, wood-floored now...broad windows looking out over the cobbled courtyard...a fireplace against the far wall that he knew from a short foray whilst waiting outside overlooked a narrow lane that led to a back garden and stable below the level of the couryard upon which stood the house itself.

"The kitchen is down a flight of stairs at the end of that hallway," said the solicitor, indicating an archway to the right of the outer wall. "It opens onto the garden in the back, and down another stair to the storage cellars below."

A SKULK OF FOXES

Nicholas nodded, saying nothing. The solicitor led him up the flight of stairs in front of them, where another room as large as the one below sprawled to his left, with an even more impressive view of the courtyard below, and less-obscured views of the towers of the New City beyond the Mews. He let himself be led through a small handful of upper rooms in the rear whose windows looked down over the garden and out across the Old City, and then up yet another fight of stairs to three smaller rooms...garret-like...snug with their own hearths...

"Your family will be arriving soon...?" asked the solicitor, whose name was Bentley.

Nicholas shook his head.

"No...it's just for me..."

Bentley seemed puzzled.

"It's rather large for one person," he suggested politely. "And one so young as yourself..."

Nicholas nodded agreeably.

"Well, Mister Bentley, one can never know what Life will bring to you..."

"That is quite true, Master Wyndham, quite true...but the monthly fee is commensurate with its size. I don't know that perhaps it will be more than you can manage...?"

Nicholas became silent again, in his mind retracing his steps through every room, each nook and niche encountered, envisioned his piano in the upstairs parlour. He took a deep breath and smiled.

"I don't want t'lease the place," he said quietly. "If it's not too costly, I think I'd like t'buy it outright if possible. Have you a selling price...?"

MICHAEL SUMMERLEIGH

Mister Bentley did indeed have a selling price, and three hours later, Master Nicholas Wyndham, twenty years old and newly arrived in the City from his home in the far northern reach of the Carillon valley a scant three days earlier, became the new owner of the old-but-newly-renovated coach house in St John's Mews. Three days after that, as carts and wagons delivered his instruments, furniture and personal belongings, he stood in the ground floor parlour and dealt with the reality of what he had done...

"I had no idea," he said. "Leaving home seemed the best thing I could do for myself. My brothers had everything in hand that needed looking after; my father seemed content t'let us 'fight' it out over who should run things when he was gone...but not in a bad way, because he let us know right away that the key to making it all work was in recognising we each had a part in it and it wouldn't work unless we worked *together*...

"But for me...for the longest time I used t'hide behind my mum, because I had no interest in the farms and our holdings, other than home being the most marvelous place in the world. Whatever it was I was supposed t'be good at, it wasn't anything I could match to my brothers' talents at running things, so I just let them have at it, and I was lucky enough that my mother made my father see that...

"So it was a year of being almost totally by myself...never going out because for the longest time I was never sure I could get by on what my parents sent every month. I knew they'd send more if I needed it, and asked for it, but I felt they'd already given enough, so I wrote music and rattled around in the coach house, re-started the garden out back...and at night

A SKULK OF FOXES

I lived with the terror of perhaps having made a dreadful mistake..."

He realised he'd been talking out loud as they walked. Yana seemed quite anxious; Ysa scarcely less so. Without "saying" as much, both conveyed a deep concern. Nicholas smiled into the dullness around them.

"...And then one day I was walking on the Promenade around the harbour and I saw this lovely blonde girl sitting on a camp-stoo, surrounded by drawings and paintings, and making charcoal sketches of everyone who passed by..."

Brandywine said Yana.

Nicholas nodded and smiled a bit more.

"Brandywine," he said. "I went back again and again and she was almost always there. I bought three of her sketches and asked if she would have some lunch with me, and then after a few days she introduced me to a sweet boy named Andrew whom she'd found sleeping in an alley....and they knew someone named Diana knew someone named Gareth who knew someone named Thomas, and all of us in our own ways were alone, cast adrift in the City, fending for ourselves. They all came to live with me at one time or another, filled up the coach house until they found places of their own...but after that I stopped feeling like I'd made any kind of mistake at all..."

Yana nipped gently at his heels, stopped them on a track between two small mountains that looked as though they'd been pounded into splinters and left to crumble into dust.

Okay now, you...? she asked, Nicholas nodded.

"Yes, okay now, me."

Ysa would go t'find Kerissa, maybe her knowing now where is your daughter. Is asking if is okay...okay...?

"I think you and I can manage for a while on our own," he said.

Yana grinned. Ysa vanished.

Chapter Sixteen – The Midnight Carnival of Souls

They had no idea what they would encounter on the far side of the river, were dismayed to find in its bleak emptiness very little to reassure them, hearten them along their way. Kerissa was certain they were heading in the right direction to rescue her father, but now found herself constantly in dread of things that had long since ceased to be a part of her life; most often her thoughts turned to Arabella, and the fact she now had no idea where to find her; that she could be in the direst of straits, mortal danger, and there would be nothing she could do to keep her from harm. Khalid seemed to know her thoughts better than she did herself.

It is this place, Kerissa Davies. It is this place where everything in all the worlds comes together...all lives...all dreams..all fears...

"I'm scared all the time, Khalid. I miss her so much I can't breathe."

You must not give the King a place in your heart. You will stop knowing how to fight back...

"That's a lot easier said than done, Khalid. Half the time I scarcely know whether I'm awake or sleeping. Everything is happening...everything feels like it could be real... and horrible all over again...and it's not even the stuff from last year..."

She was not at all in any physical distress, in spite of trudging along barefoot, without a stitch of clothing between her and what should have been, to all appearances, an extremely *un*comfortable place to be in any circumstance. She felt impervious to the rush of wind that flung dust and debris at her; unaware that drenching rain turned her head of curls into a sodden mass hanging down around her shoulders. Khalid was uncomplaining, stoically bearing each and every turn of adversity they encountered, as if aware that the true struggle of their progress was being waged in the heart and mind of his human companion. They scrambled up a barren hillside and halfway to the top of it, Kerissa turned to look back along the way they had come. They went on again, crested the hill and after a quick glance to what lay below, looked back again.

"We just crossed the Findhorn, Khalid," she said wonderingly, "and the town below us is Linden, I'm sure of it...but it's different...and it's before all the bridges got built over the river because the one at Linden was the first..."

While it seemed to be valid assumption, Kerissa at the same time recognised that the town she had taken to be Linden in many ways bore no resemblance to the town she'd been to on numerous occasions, but most recently only seen in passing, on horseback as she and Arabella had returned to the City from the Westvales the previous summer.

In the day/night she now inhabited the town appeared to be lit in a sulphurous light, and the fairgrounds on the far side of the town in a nebulous shifting haze through which she could see a massive round something outlined against the sky, that revolved endlessly, lit by dozens of flickering lamps spaced along its perimeter to mark the small carriages between the two

A SKULK OF FOXES

outer wheels. If she listened carefully, there was music heard faintly as well, but all of it discordant and unsettling.

All things here are strange mirrors of themselves as you have known them said Khalid matter-of-factly.

Kerissa shook her head, ran fingers through a rain-sodden curl that had stayed sodden amongst the rest of them, shook her head again until their rustle sounded like what she was used to hearing from them.

"You guys...sometimes you make all the sense in the world...and other times I have no idea what you're talking about."

She could feel the little dog-fox grinning.

Am saying only that here, all things are mirrors of themselves as you have known them in the stream of Life you have lived. This place can be here *even when it is gone elsewhere.*

Kerissa sighed and started down the far side of the hill, noticing that the lowering sky before them had become a roil of dense cloud sailing past sister suns that shed no light worth the name; that now the sky itself provided what little illumination there was to be found other than what the town itself managed, until the suns faded into the clouds as she watched, replaced by something large...unhealthy...that rose up like a beacon lighting the way to something dire and unfriendly.

"I'm tired," she said, frightened to hear the resignation in her own voice. "I miss 'Bella and my mom and my dad and all of this is just so wrong..."

The moonstone on her forefinger seemed dull and lifeless, its earlier brightness, that had sustained them through the dark reaches of the under-ground, gone to a desperation she could not understand. She realised she was babbling to the little fox at her feet, almost in tears.

Trust in what you have known, Kerissa Davies, not what you see here...

<hr />

As they approached the town, Kerissa's unease deepened, and deepened further when they began to encounter the inhabitants, who, though dressed themselves, seemed totally unconcerned and oblivious to the fact that she walked through their midst naked but for a silver-set moonstone ring on her left hand. Even Khalid, ever the stoic when faced with mystery or something not yet in his experience, seemed to be unsettled by the bemused expressions of the people they encountered, most of them on their way to the fairgrounds, energised in a horrible parody of anticipation.

As they drew closer, as the travesty of festive music became clearer, Khalid leapt into Kerissa's arms and stayed there, his nose twitching about in every direction, obviously as uncomfortable as Kerissa herself. Something two-footed and quite small darted out of an alleyway onto the cobblestones of the high street, collided with Kerissa's knees, bounced off them and landed before them on her bum, bawling soundlessly. Kerissa knelt beside her, concerned, and then recoiled as she realised she was looking at herself...a child of perhaps two or three summers...

...Unhappy...the entirety of la famille Boulevardiers *gathered in the ground floor front parlour of the coach house in St John's Mews, all in breathless attendance, waiting upon the birth of a child to Nicholas and Brandyine.*

A SKULK OF FOXES

Her mother was upstairs with Aunt Brandy and Uncle Nicky, being versed in midwifery and the unofficial in-charge-of-everything where newborn children was concerned. Her father was deep in conversation with Uncle Thomas; her aunt Diana looking after her cousins Edmund (a little bit older than herself) and Sebastian (a year younger) whilst Uncle Andrew was giving hugs away to Alain.

No one seemed to be taking any notice of her. No one seemed to care at all that Kerissa was left out...ignored...

She wandered into the hallway and reached up to the door latch to let herself out into the courtyard...looked left and right and up into the trees where all the cats sat transfixed, eyes unwaveringly upon the music room windows, as if they too were in attendance only to celebrate the arrival of someone new to the family. She pouted at no one and stumped angrily round to the narrow lane that led into the garden and stable behind the coach house...down steps one at a time—always careful as she'd been taught to be—and then to wandering around in silent tears...until she found a mysterious round hole at the far end and crawled into it, now beyond all care of her dress or her bare knees scraping on the ceramic of the drainage culvert she emerged into sunlight and a place she had never been...

At first there was excitement—a street she had never seen before...people and faces who looked down at her with curiosity, but went along their way without a word because giving any thought to a small child wandering alone on a side-street of the City, while not something encountered every day, still was not so noteworthy as to merit their own involvement.

Kerissa tottered along, unsure whether or not this was an adventure to be savoured, or endured as a further source of two-year old misery. Time was of no meaning and very little consequence to her; she snuffled along pavement and cobbled streets and in time came to an imposing structure that she recognised...a church that was always there whenever her mother and father brought her to visit her aunt and uncle. She stumped back along the laneway and into the courtyard, where all the cats now seemed to be in a fever of exitement...let herself back into the hallway she'd left hours earlier...

"There you are!" cried Gareth her father. "Kerissa come...you have a new cousin..."

She let herself be scooped up and transported upstairs...all the while resisting the urge to lash out...squirm her way free of her father's arms, because inwardly she knew she'd been gone forever and no one had even noticed.

He set her down beside a large bed she'd slept in many times before, but now her Aunt Brandy was propped against a mountain of pillows and her face was a little bit like she'd been crying but she was all soft and everyone around her was smiling at the strange little thing in her arms, with a tiny tiny face and a tiny mouth that made slurping noises as it sucked at the nipple of Aunt Brandy's breast...and her aunt looked so tired and so happy and Uncle Nicky looked so scared and so relieved and everyone there was looking at her now, even silly Edmund and his baby brother Sebastian...and her mother urging her closer and closer until she was right up beside her Aunt Brandy and she heard her asking:

"Would you like to hold her,'Rissa ? This is Arabella..."

She looked at the funny little creature in Brandy's arms, tried to take a step backwards but found too many grown-ups in her way. She leaned forward, curiosity now something more

A SKULK OF FOXES

important than being angry. She nodded cautiously, and found a small bundle in her arms...

"Make sure to keep her head from falling back, 'Rissa. She's very small..."

Kerissa did as she was told, made sure to cradle the head of the small thing in her arms, looked down into a tiny face framed by pale golden curls and two shiny little green eyes that felt like they had looked upon her forever and a day before they had ever met. A tiny hand grasped one of her fingers and it made a small sound that drove away all the feelings of being left out and ignored. She looked up ay Brandywine...

"Can I have her? she asked. "I want her to be mine..."

...And when she looked down at herself sprawled on the cobblestones, she was gone, the street lamplit as from Hell and, with Khalid, they stood like a standing stone battered by the tide of humanity passing them by. Kerissa realised she was weeping as if her heart would break.

※

They came to the fairgrounds, a shadow of the times when she and 'Bella and their parents had taken them there as children, brought them to the bright and joyous harvest-time fair where magicians made magic and charlatans made magic, and magic was so easily found when you were so small that it was easy to expect your life to be filled with it from that moment on.

As they made their way through throngs of fair-goers, Kerissa found Arabella in her heart, clinging to her hand half in fear—begging her older sister to look after her—and half in the crazy abandon that she would learn was an integral part of her beloved's nature, the imperative to go hell-for-leather into adventure.

She whispered, as she always whispered no matter where she was...no matter what kind of nightmare came to enfold her...

I love you 'Bella...

And found the sumptuosity of *'Bella* to be the anchor of her life, because she could imagine nothing better than being lost in her forever.

They came to the fairground then. She and Khalid, shivering somewhat because his knowledge of the strangeness that made human beings still was well short of any true comprehension; that Life was entirely much more complicated for those who walked on two feet than it could ever be for those with the luxury of moving on four.

"It wasn't me, Khalid," she said. "It was a child who looked like me, but she'd not ever been given a chance to learn...to be in love...and she never will...and now my heart is so sad..."

The dog-fox made only sympathetic foxy sounds, not knowing anything else he could offer to lessen her sadness. Once again surrounded by the crush of people who had swarmed past them earlier, Kerissa wandered cautiously, recognising the smell of roasted chestnuts gone slightly off, the sound of carousel music half a note entirely off-key, the cries of children racing past them in every direction, as if in flight from something rather than intent on the excitement of a new whirligig ride, or the small enclosure where skeletal goats and sheep and rabbits waited and wailed for the attention Kerissa once had wanted on a day that had changed her life.

A SKULK OF FOXES

They moved past a fun-house, heard the strident call of the barker inviting them inside. She paused long enough to look into a mirror beside the doorway, and fled away in horror at what she'd seen, clutching Khalid even more tightly in her arms...came at last to the great pair of wheels rising up into the sky and the hordes waiting patiently to be carried aloft in the carriages between them, each illuminated by a lamp whose flames leapt and danced in mockery of those carried upwards into the night, to the docking station high above them...and the walkway leading them all to the top of an adjacent tower. Kerissa tried to turn away, knowing full well what would happen next, but found herself gazing upward in a horrible fascination as those who had ridden the wheel two hundred feet into the air leapt from the tower...soundlessly...their arms flung wide to embrace the dark...hands fluttering in the wind of their downward passage and each face wreathed in shadows bearing an expression of such utter resignation that she had to turn away, or become as emptied of Hope as the the ruined lives that had brought them there.

Some seemed to be swallowed soundlessly up into the aether, never even reaching the ground before they winked out of existence; others could be heard to wail in thin ghost-like voices before they became featureless masses of shattered dead flesh scattered across the ground at the base of the tower. Attendants in clown-faces and brightly-coloured work clothes toiled there, shifting the detritus of souls with no future alive or dead to the beds of small carts drawn by emaciated horses with scarlet eyes and the rasp of Despair blowing out in clouds from their nostrils. Kerissa felt as if she were going mad.

This is where we must be whispered Khalid, desperately.

Kerissa closed her tightly and nodded.

"I know," she said. "I just never imagined there were people who could live lives so empty that there was nothing for them to hope for or believe in, before or after."

We do not know of such things...our living is simple...your kind have lost kindness...

"I know," she said again. "It's so wrong of me t'just want t'wish myself and 'Bella away from all of this...but I do...and the longer we stay here, the more scared I get when I think of my da...and what it must've been like that he would come here by choice, with no promise at all that he could ever be with my mom again."

She turned away from the wheel, saw a small chocolate-coloured girl staring at her from the shadows of a billowy silk tent across the way...who raised a small hand to bid her farewell before the shadows swallowed her. The air in front of them became a mad coruscation of itself, and a vixen with a small white patch on her chest stood placidly before them. Khalid leapt from Kerissa's arms to nuzzle at his older sister, easily seen to be conferring with her before Ysa turned to Kerissa.

This is Caracosh... she said. *...or a semblance of Caracosh as it would show itself to you. The one you call Nicholas...Windy...*

"Bella's father."

Ysa dipped her head once.

Yes. For now he is safe on his own path in this place. Yana is with him, and slowly all of us grow into what we must be in order to win our way back to the lives we know...

"Have you found 'Bella? My father or my mother? D'you know where they are?"

A SKULK OF FOXES

Ysa shook her head.

Arabella is lost to me. She does not need to travel through the gates, only to go where her path leads her. Your father is gone between and Zoraya has followed him. We cannot follow them if we wish to come back...

"I don't understand, Ysa."

Arabella is different explained Khalid. *She can go from one world to the next as she pleases, whenever and wherever...and your parents now have gone to where she can only bring them back to this place...*

Kerissa shivered. "They can't be anywhere anymore except here?"

Ysa shook her muzzle up at her.

They cannot go back to our side, but if Arabella can find them in-between, then they can be brought to find a place on this side that is better.

"I still don't understand," whispered Kerissa, "but can we help 'Bella... somehow...?"

Nicholas has said that where he is on his own path is in some way a familiar place for him...the Emerald Gardens as a mirror of what he has known...

Kerissa thought out loud.

"So Uncle Windy thinks Caracosh can be a mirror of our own world...on our own side of the gates...?"

Ysa nodded, for a moment falling back into the pattern of speech she and her siblings had used when they were new.

Is thinking this, him... she said.

Kerissa gave a moment of thought to the possibility and breathed a long sigh of something that might have been relief.

"We have t'go this way then...t'find the Bone Castle..."

Having crossed what she herself had recognised to be the Findhorn, and come to the darker side of what was Linden Faire in the wasteland called Caracosh, she turned and pointed to what would have been south had they not been standing in the middle of nightmare.

"Qaraq-al-Ossa...the Bone Castle...it's in the City..." she said wonderingly.

Ysa smiled...

I will tell Nicholas to meet you there.

...and vanished....

Chapter Seventeen – Brandywine Thinks Magick

The house in St John's Mews was like an armed camp in every way save for a notable lack of weapons capable of perpetrating murder and mayhem. The extended family that was *les Boulevardiers* came and went over the course of the next day, but at all times an outsider would have seen in each of them a taut wariness, as if they were ready, at any moment, to rise up in some sort of communal defense, or charge off in rescue-mode.

As she had done just over six months before, Alexandra Wyndham took over the day-to-day workings of the household, looking after meals and providing the necessaries for everyone else as they came and went about as much business-as-usual as could be managed under the circumstances. Once again, the twins became permanent residents, pitching in wherever they could, but always in such a way that there was no doubt the strain of maintaining a cheery outlook was wearing away at them.

When Andrew and Alain were gone from the house, Stella tended to stay close to Grammy Alex in order keep busy, helping out in the kitchen and tidying up after everyone. With Sebastian off at whiles to take his brother's place at the palace, Jamie tagged along after Windy's father, but often found it was in Brandy's company where he could unburden himself of worry without being embarrassed about it. Drawn by some horrific noises he'd not encountered before, he found her in her studio, bent over Nicholas' cello with a combined look of immense frustration and determination on her face. He watched quietly from the doorway for a minute or so as she bowed at the strings, and thereby learned the source of the tortured sounds that had drawn him there.

"Hi Annie Branny whatcha doin'?" he asked quietly, in a moment of silence.

Brandywine looked up, startled out of her concentration.

"Hi, Jamie…"

"You tryin' t'learn how t'play?"

She smiled. "No, not really…"

Jamie tilted his head to one side and thought about that, trying to puzzle out why Brandywine was hidden away from all the others, doing dreadful things to Uncle Windy's cello when she *wasn't* trying to learn how to play it. Brandy saw the look on his face and laughed.

"Silly, huh?"

Jamie shrugged. "I dunno," he said cautiously. "Maybe…?"

"D'you remember when Windy and Zori saved us from the Antillians last year…when Zori made the river go all-over crazy on their ships…and Windy helped…with this…?"

Jamie nodded.

"Well…he'd done what he did then once before, a long time before you and Stel were even born, and I was just tryin' t'make that same kind of magical sound."

"How come?"

"I think I need t'be able t'do it if I'm gonna help Windy help 'Rissa and 'Bella and Gareth."

A SKULK OF FOXES

"What about 'Rissa's mom? I think I understand what you guys explained about how come she's not here anymore, but maybe if you get the magical thing right you could maybe get her t'come home too, like she did with 'Bella?"

Jamie got woeful, and Brandy got woeful right along with him, setting the cello down carefully and drawing him closer for a hug. She could feel him wriggle and shiver a tiny bit, the way he always did when struggling not to cry where anyone would see him.

"It's okay, honey," she whispered, "you don't have t'be ashamed. Crying's all right. After a while it makes you feel better."

He burrowed himself deeper into her arms and she could feel her front getting wet with his silent tears. After a while he grew quiet again, but stayed where he was, comfortable if not happy.

"Can I help?" came a muffled question.

This time Brandy shrugged and Jamie sighed. "I don't know where t'put my fingers or how t'do any of it properly. Uncle Windy knows. Not me."

Jamie came away from her, rubbing at his eyes and nose with the sleeve of his shirt.

'I know about the fingers," he said.

"You do?!?!" said Brandy, incredulous.

Jamie nodded.

"When Uncle Windy was helpin' Zori he was tryin' t'do what you were doin'...tryin' to remember the first time you said about. I watched him. The sounds he made weren't as horrible as yours, but it took a while for him t'figure it out all over again...and then he *did* figure it out...I saw him grin...and when he made the next sound I could feel almost everything all around go shivery."

"Jamie, can you show me where he put his fingers?"

He nodded. "Sure. I remember..."

He picked up the cello and slowly pointed at the two bass strings, and the places on the fingerboard where he had seen Nicholas' fingers on the day he'd helped Zoraya rouse the earth from sleep.

Brandywine cautiously moved the bow across the strings and the cello made more horrible sounds.

"You might have t'say magic words, too," he said.

Brandy looked chagrined.

"I don't know know any magic words, Jamie."

"I remember them, too."

"Jamie you're a miracle, what'd Windy say?"

"They might not be real magic words."

"Just tell me, okay?"

Jamie nodded. "He said *Work, dammit, work!* ... in this really ferocious voice, and after that everything was swell."

Brandy started laughing, and Jamie got another round of hugs for his trouble that he seemed to enjoy quite a bit, but when Brandywine tried bowing the strings again *and* using the magic words along with, the results were still a lot less than bearable.

"I don't think I'm ever gonna get this t'go right," she said unhappily.

"Am I allowed t'try, Branny? I think maybe you weren't holding the bow good. You have t'hold on to it, but not too tight so it sort of floats on the strings all by itself."

A SKULK OF FOXES

Brandywine offered bow and cello in outstretched hands; Jamie accepted them gingerly and then said he might need some help holding the cello while he put his fingers where he thought they should go. Brandy steadied it for him, and a moment later a real sound rumbled through her studio. Jamie frowned.

"It's not right," he said. "It's almost right...but the second string is too high."

"I know how t'do that part," said Brandywine. "Do what you just did and I'll try t'fix it."

Again Jamie let the bow float across the strings, but this time she gave the tuning peg a wee small almost-quarter turn to loosen the one in need of work...and as Jamie drew the bow back again both of them felt the floor move a little bit under their feet.

"You did it!" she cried. "Jamie...Jamie you did it..."

"I did," he said, looking proud and totally stunned at the same time.

"When you and me get Uncle Windy home you should tell him you wanna be a musician just like him!"

"I do?" he said, looking proud and totally stunned at the same time.

Brandy nodded, and started thinking about how their real work was about to begin.

Chapter Eighteen – The House on the Borderland

The most unnerving thing about watching her reality fall apart was the silence that came with its dissolution. Suddenly, her shadow-steed was gone and Arabella was on her knees, seemingly floating in the middle of nothingness that was not even blackness so much as it was a simple lack of any colour at all. Just as quickly, all of the nothingness disappeared and what replaced it seemed so familiar, so *normal*, that she thought she somehow had managed to reason her way back through the gates into her own world.

What surrounded her now seemed like the Westvales she remembered, an idyllic worldscape of bright colours and living things that felt like they were bursting with energy…waiting to be reborn…trembling with the anticipation of newness… The only thing that might have been in the least bit disturbing was that she could find no sun in the sky above her, or clouds, or anything at all to mar the surface of its opalescent splendour. It seethed gently above her, casting a soothing warmth down upon everything that moved beneath it.

I must've taken a wrong turn somewhere she thought, *but it seems like any time I'm expecting something I always end up with something entirely different. This is a big improvement though…*

A SKULK OF FOXES

The pastoral quality of her new reality went on forever in every direction, and in those first moments she couldn't imagine a better place to be if you were bent on wandering around on the other side of your old reality. She soon found the only down side in all of comfortable newness was what hung on the belt around her hips—a dueling sword and two daggers that, drawn out of their sheaths for inspection, became wraith-like...wispy... as if they didn't really exist at all. Arabella became apprehensive.

"They're no use here,' she said. "I hope there's a good reason for that...like maybe I don't need them just now...nobody around in need of whacking or ventilation...?"

She managed to put them away where they belonged, picked an horizon and started walking towards it, moving her thoughts away from disaster and letting her bare feet do some luxuriating in the cool grass. She climbed a low rise and found a massive stone house nestled into a hillside half a mile away.

I'll likely be a lifetime getting there she thought *but it's pretty much the way things work these days. I hope everyone's okay waiting for me t'save them all...*

She reached the house a lot faster than she'd ever imagined she would, stood at the iron-hinged wooden door and banged away for a minute or so before it opened and she shared a bit of surprise with the person who'd opened it.

"Father Ambrosius...?"

'Not anymore," he said, looking at her curiously. "You're Arabella, aren't you...? What on earth are you doing here?"

"I could ask you the same question," she said.

Ambrosius smiled. "Yes of course you may, and I've had glimpses of lives where I was Ambrosius...but I'm Teodor Alexeyev... you *do* remember, yes?"

Arabella smiled and nodded. "I do...and you've been missed..."

"I've done what I could. It's taken some doing and quite a bit of it is rather confusing... yet I do seem to remember it was your mother who gave *my* life back to me. What have you been up to...?"

"I guess I was dead for a little while."

Alexeyev nodded. "Yes...I'd heard that too, was I hoping you might come my way so I could turn you in the right dirction...and Zoraya, I heard that—"

"She brought me back."

"Yes."

Both stood awkwardly on the doorstep, Alexeyev in some plain canvas trousers and a linen shirt embroidered with a strange bird no one could name taking flight from the bell of an hibiscus flower.

"Mister Alexeyev what are you doin' here?"

"It's my job now...waiting here to make sure nobody goes on by accident," he said soberly. "Living on the edge."

"The edge of what?"

'You know the answer to that very well, Arabella. Why are *you* here?"

"Zori's magic...and the flower... the stuff that brought me back, it started things up again. Gareth went looking for her the same way Mister Robertson went looking for his lost Rochelle and then...well...I guess it was never as simple as any of us thought it would be..."

A SKULK OF FOXES

"It happens that way quite often," he said softly. "Why don't you come inside, my dear. I'll make tea and you can tell me whatever you please, and then I can point you in the direction you're looking for.'

"*That* would be wonderful, Mister Alexeyev. I keep thinking I should hurry things up a bit, though, if I'm t'be of any help..."

"I won't keep you all that long, my dear."

The round little man who had been Father Ambrosius just smiled and took her in hand, led her into the coolth and comfort of the great stone house, down a short stone-floored hallway into a drawing room full of brocades and *knick-knacks anciens,* all warmed by a small fire crackling away on the hearth.

"You've grown up a lot, Arabella. When *I* died in your world you were a very grown-up girl, but now you're a very grown-up young woman."

"Mister Alexeyev—"

"Teodor is fine, Arabella. I'm not nearly so formal as I used to be."

'Bella sat on a big stuffed sofa, drew her feet up and realised she was very tired, but that here in Teodor Alexeyev's house she felt completely safe.

"I can't stay very long," she said, wishing she could stay forever and wait for everyone she loved to find her.

"I know, my dear. I'll make tea this very instant, tell you and show you what you need to know, and then send you on your way."

Gratefully, Arabella nodded and closed her eyes. When she opened them again, round Mister Alexeyev was pouring tea into porcelain cups and buttering a bit of pastry that looked as though it might just have come out of his oven.

"How are those two boys?" he asked "I think remember that I frightened that poor Andrew fellow quite badly...and then he met someone...Alain...?"

Arabella nodded and said, "They're fine, Mis...Teodor. They adopted twins a few years ago...Jamie and Stella. You don't need t'feel badly about Andrew, though...

Alexeyev's face grew thoughtful, his eyes going a bit blank as he searched through his lifetimes.

"I was very intolerant...acting against everything I came to learn was truly important. It's never really bothered me here, but I recall Andrew from...somewhere... and I was quite cruel to him."

"You should forgive yourself then. When I was little and realised that I was gonna love Kerissa forever, I went to Andrew and told him, and I asked him if maybe I was doing something bad. He told me all about going into the crypt under the church...

"He said he was really upset by some of the things you said t'him...and frightened too...but he also said it made him angry...stubborn...and it gave him the courage t'stop doubting himself...and then he met Alain, and they brought the twins home and now they're all doing fine."

"That's why you're here then, to make sure it stays that way, for them and everyone else?"

"I guess so. Is that why I'm here?"

She took an offered cup and saucer and gratefully sipped at the steaming tea, pretending for a moment she was home with her mother and father and...everyone...

A SKULK OF FOXES

"I need to be in a place called Qaraq-al-Ossa," she said. "I need t'find the Bone Castle and bring Gareth back...and make sure my da and 'Rissa are okay too. It's such a long story. I was gonna do it all alone, but Hasan's babies brought them after me. You remember Hasan? Zori's magical fox...?"..."

Alexeyev nodded, but then his round face grew pensive as he sipped at his own cup. He put it down on the small table between them and reached for her hand.

"You're too late to bring Gareth back to your side of the gates, Arabella," he said sadly. "Gareth went in-between, and no one living can do that and go back to the same life they left behind. *In-between* is an end for everything we know of this place we live in and all the things we know nothing about. The souls with nowhere to go find themselves there, but if he doesn't belong and you find him...if you bring him back from in-between, then he must stay in a reality on this side of the gates, never go back to yours."

"Mom says we all go back into *something*...and then we get t'come back..."

"This is a truth, Arabella...your mother has always been so much more wise than anyone has ever given her credit for...but for those of us who have not been able to be what we should have been, sometimes it's a very long journey back from wherever it is we go..."

She took another sip of her tea.

"I should go now."

Alexeyev nodded.

"First I must show you where you are going, and explain just a little bit more..."

MICHAEL SUMMERLEIGH

He took her hand again, led her back into the entrance hall and down a flight of stairs. At the bottom was another hallway, at its end a second heavy wooden door, studded with iron, bolted in three places. Alexeyev drew all three bolts, one at a time, and opened the door slowly onto a small stone balcony overlooking the place she was looking for.

"There is another door below that will open upon this place, Arabella," he said, "but stay a bit longer and let me tell you something of what you will find. Caracosh is where you're going…and Qaraq-al-Ossa…the Bone Castle…is at its heart, where all the infinite lives and worlds and realities in the universe converge."

Arabella wondered that the place Alexeyex named Caracosh should lie below them, when she was quite certain he'd taken her underground in his home to unlock the door behind them. She turned to him in puzzlement and he smiled reassuringly.

"Just accept this, my dear. The challenge will come when you have actually arrived in Caracosh. I ventured there, out past my doors…but only once, and truly feared I might never return.

"You see, there is an underlying…spirit, I suppose…of Chaos that rules there, taking many forms but most often styling itself as a king in tattered yellow robes. If you encounter him…it…always be wary, because he, like the land he holds in his sway, will quite often show you what you most wish to see, so that it seemingly can be dashed away from you in an instant if you don't know the way things work there."

Arabella looked past his outstretched hand and down upon the City, bathed in summer. The Findhorn wound its

A SKULK OF FOXES

way through to the sea, diamonds flashing over its progress as spray leapt into the air and captured sunlight one breath at a time. Lambent bits of stone in the granite battlements of the Amaranth Palace did the same, jade curtains showered down along the forested paths of the Emerald Gardens, glanced blindingly off the glass and steel towers of the New City. Far off in the haze beyond the City she caught small darting glimpses of more forest, and farmland bursting with new life already racing for the time of harvest and the quiet sleep of winter. Beneath all of it ran a current of something she knew was the voice of the life-river of the earth in her time and place. And in the paradise of her heart she felt her family at peace in all of it.

"It's perfect, but it's not real," she whispered. "That's what you're saying, isn't it...that I have t'be careful not t'get lost in it?"

She couldn't take her eyes from her dream of perfection, dared not look at Alexeyev lest the image fall apart in front of her eyes, as so many already had done. She felt him nodding his head beside her.

"Arabella, I've learned that *real* is very much what we choose it to be. Reality for most of us has come to include the presence of the others just like us, all dreaming much the same dream and so it's our combined effort that holds it all together; then there are the ones who cannot see it, or want something so utterly different that they go mad with want of it. If you trust in what you now see too deeply, if you wish for it with too much of that which has made it real on your side of the gates, when you arrive in Caracosh, the Chaos will likely steal it away from you, and you will end this lifetime mourning a loss that never occurred.

MICHAEL SUMMERLEIGH

"Does that make *any* sense to you?"

"Mostly it makes all the sense in the world, Mister Alexeyev. The dream I live in with 'Rissa... my mom and my da...all my friends...

"You're saying Caracosh is where our hearts and all our hopes begin...and it's where they can just as easily die if we start thinking we're entitled to them just because we can dream them at all..."

Alexeyev nodded.

"Mostly that's it exactly. So I imagine it *is* time for you to go, my dear. It's been a true and wondrous pleasure to meet you again for the first time, Arabella. Travel safely..."

When she was gone, he watched her for while, trudging off into the cruelty of Caracosh, never looking back, and utterly oblivious to the horrible thing that had happened to her. He managed to dredge up memories of the little girl who used to toddle around the Mews, climb up the steps to the church...show him Light and Innocence in much the same fashion as the day her mother had dragged him off to meet his "God".

He watched her go away, and when he could no longer see her, the last fading image of her on the ridge above Caracosh, turning to wave at him, he wept for her, and what he knew would be the price of her unlimited love and devotion.

Part Three

THE BONE CASTLE

Chapter Nineteen – Brandywine Takes a Turn at Magick

Stella was huffy. She sat at the downstairs kitchen table drinking hot chocolate with Grampa Fred while Grammy Alex washed dishes and made certain dinner would be ready for everyone when the day was done.

Diana was off to her digs to teach a dance class. Uncle Thomas had gone to lend a hand to Alain and Andrew at the warehouse and markets on Water Street. Sebastian was at the Amaranth Palace, filling in for his brother who was supposed to be wandering round the Westvales in service to the cute guy everyone called King Evrard, but most likely was simply staying in Bedford for a while, with that nice lady named Darya Adair.

Her huffiness came from the fact that Jamie—who under normal circumstances was an inseparable and often crazy-making addition to her life—had been, over the last day or so, nowhere in sight, instead closeted with Annie Branny way upstairs in the garret room she used for her painting studio. This was unacceptable.

On the other hand, it had been a long stretch of years since Frederick Wyndham had dealt with anyone under the age of eight, but it was obvious that Stella was in need of some sort of companionship, and she'd been spending a lot of time following him around, doing pretty much the same thing he

A SKULK OF FOXES

himself had found himself doing—keeping busy just because. He popped a little marshmallow into her chocolate from across the table, tried for two in a row, but Stella knocked it onto the floor and made a great show of her huffiness.

"What's what, Stella?" asked Frederick. His three eldest sons back in the Carillon had almost a double handful of grandchildren amongst them, but it was here in the City, surrounded by the *family* of his youngest son, that he found himself most inclined to be grandfatherly in any capacity.

"You're looking like a thundercloud."

Stella raised up her head, startled, shook her mop of dark curls and remained grumpily silent.

"You know it can make your face turn inside out if you stay cranky for any great length of time....and sometimes the cranky stays on your face on both sides so you can never get rid of it."

Stella looked at Grampa Fred like he'd lost his mind.

"You're being silly."

Frederick nodded enthusiastically.

"Of course...but I still want t'know why you're so upset."

"It's Jamie," she said.

"Okay. Jamie. What's he done that's so terrible?"

"He always tells me everything, just like I always tell *him* everything...'cept now he's gone all secret squirrel with Annie Branny..."

"They're up t'something."

"They are! And Jamie's not sayin'..."

"That's all it is?"

"That's plenty, Grampa..."

Frederick Wyndham hoped his smile didn't show.

"What're we gonna do t'fix it?"

153

Stella went for major huffy.

"I don't care!"

"Sure you do. I'll help. What're we gonna do?"

"I wanna know what's what! How come he's not sayin'..."

Frederick Wyndham nodded thoughtfully, called out softly for his wife.

"Alex we need a bit of help here..."

Alexandra turned away from the sink, drying her hands and undoing an apron from her waist. She wandered over to the table and sat beside Stella, raised eyebrows at her and her husband.

"Jamie's been keeping secrets from Stella, about what he's been up to with Brandy. It's not happened before and she's not happy with it."

Alexandra hoped *her* smile didn't show. She dragged the girl onto her lap and did her best to smother her with a hug.

"Then maybe we better find out what's going on, because we can't have Stella being huffy."

"I'm not bein' huffy, Gramma—"

"Just in case then," said Alexandra. "Let's go see what we can do about all the reasons you're not bein' huffy."

She got Stella on her feet beside the table, stood up beside her and looked at Frederick as if to say *Come along then, my love, we'd best look after this now rather than later...*

―❦―

Alexandra made sure everything on the stove was in no danger of becoming cinders, and then they trooped upstairs, Stella a bit more energetically than either of her adoptive grandparents. When they were again a threesome, on the small landing

A SKULK OF FOXES

providing entrance to the trice of small attic rooms, there could be discerned, albeit faintly, a slow cautious rumbling sound that in all likelihood was someone messing about with Windy's cello. Stella knocked imperiously, emboldened by the presence of her newly-recruited allies, and Brandy's voice bid them enter...

It was a small room, lit entirely with daylight streaming like honey through a broad skylight overhead, redolent with the smell of linseed oil, turpentine and paint...filled with a controlled chaos of canvases against the walls, a few properly hung, and charcoal sketches strewn everywhere including the drawing table in the far corner. Brandywine sat poised on a low stool in front of a canvas that was at least as tall as herself by two-to-three feet wide. Jamie sat in a chair beside her, with Windy's cello before him, and the bow hovering over its strings.

Addressing her daughter-in-law, Alexandra said, "We've come to uncover the mystery of your secret squirreling...or whatever it is you call it...because Stella is in no way being huffy about not knowing anything about it."

Jamie appeared to be slightly put out by this, but Brandywine, with a handful of brushes spiking out from the clustered knot of her hair, and one poised over her canvas, seemed relieved.

"Thank goodness," she said. "Me and Jamie was going witless with trying t'do magick. We need help. It worked like all get-out when Nicky and Zori were at it, but me and Jamie could use some extra."

She reached a hand to Stella, who promptly ensconced herself in her arms and put her tongue out in her twin's direction. Jamie appeared slightly more put out than a moment before.

"Me and Annie Branny are doin' stuff, Stel. Maybe I'm gonna be a musician like Uncle Windy but right now we got more important things to work on. It's not girl stuff."

Frederick and Alexandra looked at Brandy, who looked at them, and then at Jamie.

"Excuse me," she said, pointedly. "The last time I looked, Jamie, I was pretty much a girl..."

Jamie did a quick review of his latest silliness and his face turned a somewhat ruddier colour than was his normal everyday complexion. He put his head down a bit, chastened, looked at his sister.

"Branny's tryin' t'make a door," he said. "I'm helping because she says if we can make the same sounds Uncle Nicky made for Zori, maybe we can give them a place where we can rescue them from wherever they've gone..."

"That's silly," said Stella.

"No, Stel, it's not silly at all. There was this guy named Robertson..."

With there no longer being a prospect of violence in the wind, Brandywine found folding stools in a closet and everyone sat down in front of her canvas.

"I don't know what I'm doing," she said unhappily. "I remember when me and Nicky found this strange canvas by Robertson—the painter who lived in the house on the laneway here, the one that Father Ambrosius took over for a shelter..."

Frederick and Alexandra nodded...

"So one day he just disappeared and he left us this note that he was goin' off t'find his lost love in wherever it was he'd

A SKULK OF FOXES

decided t'go...but the painting was like a doorway and me and Nicky figured he'd just walked into his painting...through one of the gates that Nicky was talking about...and then there was this time when Zori took us to a dreamland palace out over the water, and Nicky said he'd seen Robertson again, and the girl he'd loved before she died, and they were finally together again..."

Alexandra looked puzzled, looked at her husband, who shrugged, as if to say *Good luck my dear I have no idea what's going on...*

"Brandy...I guess now there's not much you can do or say to surprise either of us...but this painting thing...and *the gates*...?"

"I'm trying t'make one, Alex...they're like doorways into another place where we're all pretty much doing what we're doing now but maybe after dinner...or yesterday...but back before me and Nicky...before he found out how much I loved him...Robertson made one so he could go back t'be with Rochelle de Montenay...so I wanna make one if I can...something we can can go through and bring everyone home. I thought if me and Jamie could make the same sort of magick that Nicky and Zori did t'save the City..."

She looked at all of them, helplessly.

"We need more than what I can give t'this. Jamie's got the notes that make everything rumble the same way as when the Findhorn went over the Antillian ships, but I've got no magick...not like what happened with Robertson...and we need more... something else I don't know what...t'make it work..."

She turned and indicated the canvas she had been working on, where in rough charcoal slashes a sylvan glade stood empty...waiting...and a framed door showed itself betwixt a pair of ancient oak trees, with a small hand in the open doorway, reaching for anyone in need of homecoming, and a courtyard just beyond....

Alexandra reached for Frederick's hand, and he said:

"How do we...all of us...help you?"

Stella stopped being huffy, took herself from Brandywine's arms and looked at her brother.

"You're tryin' t'bring everyone home?"

Jamie nodded.

"'Kay then..." she said. "Tell what we gotta do..."

❧

After supper, it became an all-night affair, with Windy's parents and Stella sitting round Jamie and Brandywine, all of them concentrating upon the same thought, almost unconscious, as Jamie cautiously bowed the cello into a soft rumble of the song that was the voice of the City and of the land itself. Every now and again, Stella's bright eyes could be seen to keek out from under lowered lids, to spark with amazement as she watched Annie Branny at work ...painting...adding colour to the charcoal slashes...with her own eyes closed.

When morning sunlight started creeping through the skylight, they awoke one by one in response to Brandy's gentle prodding, inviting them all downstairs to breakfast. Stella hung back for a moment as the others trooped off, an instant to look underneath the linen draped over the canvas that Brandy had worked on all night. A frown of puzzlement gave way to breathless surprise as she reached a tentative finger to its surface; then she hurried off to catch up to the others.

Chapter Twenty – The End in Sight Maybe

They trudged on in the general direction of what Nicholas had surmised to have been Qaraq-al-Ossa. Ysa's coming and going was no less unsettling than it had ever been, but he was beginning to comprehend the nature of the alternate realities that Thraxus had postulated thousands of years earlier, beginning to recognise the *quirkiness* of the way they worked, always in some way linked to his own personal perceptions of everything around him. In essence, he had begun to trust his own instincts when it came to dealing with them, so while the possibility of reaching the Bone Castle seemed to have been removed from the immediate horizon, he and Yana continued on in the staunch belief they were on the right road.

Their faith in this belief seemed to become more and more justified as they went on, the wasteland giving way to the rabbit-warren streets of a phantom city as they came to the end of what Nicholas had surmised to be the rotting corpse of the Emerald Gardens. For a time he and Yana wandered in circles, followed by unseen eyes staring out from upper-storey windows, or small packs of homeless mongrels who looked at them hungrily before Nicholas would drive them off with his staff. At other times they would see half-starved children peering out from doorways and alleys, with eyes every bit as hungry as those of the pye-dogs; or adults who crept along beside them with the empty shells of the buildings lining the streets at their backs, weighing the chance of a successful predation, and what might come to them for the effort.

"Good thing I'm such an imposing specimen," Windy remarked wryly. "Who knows what kind of mischief they'd be up to if I looked a tad less dangerous."

Nicholas is making a joke, yes...? asked Yana.

"Nicholas is making a joke," he laughed. "But look over there, Yana," he said, reaching down so he could perch her on his shoulder. "That must be where we're going. It's where the Amaranth Palace would be if we'd not decided on a holiday in Hell."

Is the Bone Castle...?

"I think so. All things considered, one could logically expect it to be so. Now it's just a matter of actually getting there in this odd place where a city block turns itself inside out and ends up being a week-long wander."

Maybe it is for us to hurry now...?

"Hurrying seems to be counter-productive at the best of times, Yana. Let's just follow our noses and when your sister gets back perhaps we can map a course for ourselves that will get us there in a hurry."

Yana made foxy *yes* noises, licked his ear and curled her tail round his neck. They stepped away from a block of row-houses into the centre of an ancient cobbled square and Yana became anxious.

Careful now, Nicholas. Something comes...

Something took shape on the other side of the square, a frenzy of the time-place continuum until it took on the

A SKULK OF FOXES

contours of a human form...darkly dressed...a face of bitterness and hatred that Nicholas remembered all too well from being a child in the Carillon...

"You can't save her, you know," it said. "Your precious cunt of a daughter. You can't save any of them..."

"You're wrong, Renard," said Nicholas Wyndham. "I can save them all, and you'll still be the pathetic corpse my cunt of a daughter made of you..."

Nicholas laughed out loud.

"Now you have nothing to say, Renard? No more empty threats from someone who can do no wrong because there's *always* someone else t'blame for you being such a pathetic piece of human garbage?"

"I'll make you suffer!"

"And when you're finished you still will have no more days in the days of your life...and I...knowing you as my father knew you...and his father before him knowing your own father....I'll have my family back and you will never...*never*....trouble us again..."

De Montenay ground his teeth...snarled...Nicholas felt himself cast backward in Time...

...At his piano...all the others asleep...on the floors...the one bed in the room he'd chosen for himself...feeling desolate...frightened...the small sense of having done some goodness for other souls as lost as himself fading away in the dreadful loneliness of having discovered friends, but not knowing any of them so well as to beg any of them to be the arbiter of his own salvation...

He played soft chords...an arpeggio and crescendo of no volume at all lest he wake them...let them see how someone can live a life so rich with Love and still be afraid... alone...so desperate for more of it...

Yana nipped his ear.

Ysa is back...

But he was still lost in the recollection...broken above the keyboard of his piano...his head bowed down over ivory keys black and white watered with tears...with a hand on his shoulder and a soft voice that said:

Don't cry, Windy. Come to bed...

Chapter Twenty One - The King's Gambit

Sebastian came awake slowly, stretching himself out to where his feet bumped against the footboard of the four-poster. He could feel the first faint light of false dawn in the windows, but found a much more interesting focus of his attention when a hand moved gently over his thigh and cupped him, and one fingernail teased him lightly to arousal.

"Are you awake?" asked Evrard.

Sebastian grinned to himself and wriggled backwards.

"I am now," he said.

"Can I have you?" asked Evrard.

"You can have me whenever you want me," said Sebastian. "You're the king..."

There were a few moments in-between one thought and its doing. Sebastian closed his eyes as he reached for the hand of his liege-lord and lover, put it to his lips and then down to where it had been at the start.

"I'm really glad I saved your life," he said softly.

"Me too," said Evrard. "Otherwise I might be dead."

"Go slow, Ev...it feels good...I love you..."

Together they moved in a small back and forth. Sebastian stopped thinking about the dawn and became lost in the lick of

Evrard's tongue on the underside of an earlobe, the light snap of his teeth on his shoulder.

"Someday this might be a problem," said the king

"Not today, though..."

"No...not today...not at all today..."

"Edmund loves her, y'know. I could tell...it had everything and nothing t'do with Robin being gone."

Evrard laughed softly.

"I knew right away," he said, rocking himself gently against the bum of his temporary looker-after of day-to-day things in the palace. "It took all of perhaps a minute or two. It's why he's in Bedford, and I can have you now...all to myself..."

"Edmund would never give you any kind of grief for this, Ev. All of us have grown up knowing the only thing that matters is to go on loving each other...it's the best way t'get by..."

"What about the girls, Sebastian...and Nicholas...Gareth and Zoraya...?

Sebastian went lost for a moment, clutching at the hand that clutched at him.

"That's for after, Evrard," he said, breathing heavily. "Just don't stop what you're doing and we'll catch up t'the world later. Besides, I don't know if there's anything we can do that's not already being done..."

Except that the royal bedchamber suddenly became chill with a rush as if every last breath of air had left the room, and Sebastian in the midst of shuddering apart in pleasure felt himself alone...turning in the instant when something leprous and clothed in yellow rags snatched Evrard away from him...

A SKULK OF FOXES

Stella brought a big plate of scrambled eggs and crispy potatoes with diced onions mixed in to table, squunched her way between Jamie and Diana and began to share the food on her plate. Jamie looked shocked. Their lives together had been a mostly-peaceful round of each one of them looking out for the other—the simple pleasure of a pleasure for one of them not being any good unless it was a pleasure for both of them—but when it came to food, for some reason, that sense of two-being-one-ness went out the door. Stella finished sharing and whispered:

"We did it, Jamie."

"What'd we do, Stel?" He looked at the crispy potatoes with suspicion.

"We helped Annie Branny. *You* helped Annie Branny. It worked."

Jamie looked impossibly proud, and crunched a potato to prove it.

"What'd I do? What worked?" he asked.

Stella leaned closer and whispered into his ear. His eyes went wide. He looked up and down the kitchen table to make sure no one was paying any attention to them. Stella said:

"I'll show you later, okay? We'll go back upstairs when everyone else is doin' other stuff..."

He nodded, and went to work on his extra breakfast. All the others at table were doing their best not to give in to the sense of helplessness that had overtaken them all in the wake of loved ones disappearing at the drop of a hat. Thomas and Diana shared a somewhat guilty sense of relief that Edmund was off wandering the Westlands with a new honey whilst Sebastian stood in his place helping things along at the palace. Alain and

Andrew seemed stricken, looking at the twins every so often and hoping that they, at least, would in no way become actively involved in the proceedings, but feeling guilty for the thought when they looked at Brandywine and Nicholas' parents. The fact that there were so many empty places at the table was worse than unsettling to all of them."

Alexandra Wyndham spoke to her daughter-in-law.

"Do you think we've done something worthwhile, Brandy?" she asked quietly.

Brandy made a doubtful face, brushed away strands of hair from where they'd clung to her lips and tried to look optimistic.

"I guess we'll find out soon enough, Alex," she said. "When we're done with breakfast I'm gonna go back upstairs and see if we managed it. I used extra dryers in my oils so we could find out maybe sooner than later."

Evrard felt the chill wind an instant before his bed and Sebastian disappeared out from under him. There was a nauseating sense of being turned upside down and sideways in total darkness, followed by an abrupt dead-stop against cold damp stone. He'd not been aware of closing his eyes, but now, in opening them, he found himself in what he had no trouble identifying as a *oubliette*, a place somewhere well below ground level where living things that had become troublesome in one way or another were sent to rot by those who had determined them to be troublesome. He'd read enough history to recognise that being bare-ass naked on cold wet stone was in a grand and ancient tradition. Somewhat of a departure from the chronicles extant of such things was the menacing figure of something

A SKULK OF FOXES

in yellow rags that stood over him, lit in silhouette by a torch raised over its head.

Jamie and Stella crept upstairs whilst the breakfast clean-up kept everyone else busy in the kitchen. In stockinged feet they climbed the last flight of stairs to Brandy's garret studio, slipped through the door and closed it quietly behind them. Stella was hopping with excitement.

"We really made some magick, Jamie," she whispered, and tiptoed to the shrouded easel that stood in a stream of morning sun beneath the skylight. Carefully, she climbed onto Brandywine's chair and stripped the linen coverlet away from the painting she had laboured over through the night, in company with those who had joined their wills to her own that something of use might be created.

"Wow!" said Jamie, staring at the painting, that was at least a head taller than himself.

"What is it?"

Stella made a face and shrugged.

"I dunno, a doorway in the middle of a forest," she said, "but when I tried t'touch it, my finger went in."

"Your finger went in what?" demanded her brother.

"The painting, Jamie...my finger went *into* the painting instead of just touching it..."

Jamie mulled that over for a few seconds.

"No way," he said.

Stella nodded.

"Go ahead. You try."

"Not me," he said taking a step backward. "If it's magical it could be dangerous."

"If it's magical it's because that's what Annie Branny was tryin' t'do. You can say whatever you want, but *I* think she made a gate...or a door...or something...like what Uncle Windy was talkin' about the other night."

"It *does* look kinda real, whatever it is," replied Jamie. "Like you could just walk right into it..."

Stella sighed and put on a weary-but-patient face for her twin, shaking her head at him.

"That's why it's magical. We can go through and save 'Bella and 'Rissa and Uncle Windy and Gareth and the foxes and everyone..."

"How d'you know that, Stella? *We* don't know anything about that stuff, except *maybe* we got some people in our family who *do* know."

"We have t'try, Jamie," she said. "Time is of the essence."

"What's that mean?"

"I think it means we gotta hurry."

Jamie sighed, did some more furious thinking. When he'd done enough of that he took his sister's hand.

"So we're just gonna walk into Annie Branny's painting?"

Stella nodded again.

"Now...?"

"Now," she said, and they did.

"...Perhaps you would care to explain," Evrard said softly. He was acutely aware that the suggestion was somewhat ludicrous given the circumstances, but for lack of anything else to say

A SKULK OF FOXES

until such time as he'd figured out what had happened, he thought the maintenance of some semblance of dignity would fill the bill; that he was cold and shivering and thoroughly unnerved by being whisked away from a long languorous morning of love-making with a close friend also factored into his stall for time.

"You are the king in this place," said the faceless voice.

"So I've been told," said Evrard, "though I must confess I would happily cede lordship over this particular corner of wherever we are to anyone who prefers life in a dank dark hole in the ground whilst being terrorised by someone such as yourself."

"You are dear to the enemies of those who would serve me...and my kingdom dies as we speak, as it has done for thousands of years."

"So what you're saying is—"

"Kings must rule kingdoms or they cease to be kings at all."

"So it's a question of lordship, then? Being in charge makes you... important... defines your existence? and so much so that it doesn't matter at all what it is you're in charge of so long as someone is kissing your ass. You want my kingdom..."

The faceless thing could be heard to smile, and Evrard began to forget that he'd promised himself not to get overly emotional too soon. The thing was imposing, entirely too confident...and there was, as well, the fact that he himself was naked and undeniably at the mercy of whatever it was had done the whisking of him from his bedchamber. The cowled shadow-face dipped once in agreement.

"And I will have it."

MICHAEL SUMMERLEIGH

"Do *you* even *have* an ass to kiss? Who...what are you that your accomplishments in stealth and thievery make you think you're entitled to rule anything?"

"You are being clever. I find it annoying."

"Well I'm sor—"

Evrard's attempted pretense of contrition was interrupted by a rush of wind and something at the end of a tattered sleeve that slammed his head into the stone wall at his back.

"Not quite yet," said his gaoler, "but you *will* be sorry...quite soon...I assure you..."

Evrard rose to his knees groggily, then to his feet.

"I hope you'll not expect me to beg you for...anything..." he said, and spat blood. "I've known a tyrant or two in my time."

"Yes...I know your father very well..."

Evrard felt breath leaving his body and Fear moving in. As he strove desperately to think/say something that could bring him back to some kind of solid footing with whatever it was that stood before him, he saw the cowled head jerk sideways, lifting the shadow where its face should have been up into the air, and heard an hiss of what he shuddered to think was pleasure.

The yellow tattered thing took one long stride towards an iron door in the far wall and faded into the last flickerings of his torchlight.

Ysa found Nicholas lost in a nightmare twenty years old, and Yana desperately trying to comfort him, bring him back from the despair that ran like lifeblood in the land named Caracosh. She and her sister exchanged frightened glances when it seemed like he had become irretrievably lost in his memories. Yana leapt forward, put her teeth into his ear, leapt away as his eyes opened with shock and pain and the return of awareness to his surroundings.

Nicholas we must go! said Ysa.

"We're almost there, Ysa," he said dazedly. "Look...you can see the castle now..."

Not there. 'Rissa will go. We must go to the place in this land that is your place in the other...

Nicholas still was too lost in nightmare to understand.

Brandywine made a gate. The children have gone through. They are on this *side now, and the king is knowing of it...*

"The children? 'Bella and 'Rissa? Edmund? Sebastian?"

The small ones...hurry...

"Jamie and Stella? But how do we hurry in this place, Ysa?"

The vixens crawled into his lap as he struggled to sit upright, drew the ragged sleeves of his shirt around them with their teeth.

We are strong enough now was all she said...

It appeared to be the courtyard in St John's Mews, but the apple trees were lifeless and dead and cats lay littered across the cobblestones like little rags of furry garbage.

Nicholas struggled to his feet, leaning upon his staff as something dire materialised on the far side of the courtyard and fell upon the two children in its centre.

What do I do? he cried to himself, recognising the sickening shroud of colour coalescing in the air before him. Ysa and Yana leapt from his arms and went for the phantasm that was become more real with every breath. Nicholas listened to the screams of Jamie and Stella as it wrenched them from the ground, each by one arm, and realised he could do no less. He heard the the king smile.

"You cannot save them."

"I won't let you have them."

Disdain filled the air of the courtyard with the stench of its disregard.

"They are mine..."

Nicholas rushed towards him.

"Not fucking yet!" he said...

...And found himself thrown against the walls of the courtyard, his upraised staff splintered in half and flung away as he lay bleeding. He struggled to regain his feet and realised his left leg was broken and the thing bent over the twins with teeth showing in the darkness of the yellow cowl was mocking him for his love...and his helplessness...as two foxes snapped and growled just out of reach...

"Leave them!" Nicholas cried. "They're nothing to you."

"But they are everything to you."

"Leave them...bastard, are you so empty you have t'feed on Fear...leave them, damn you! Can't I feed your hatred enough?"

The creature smiled in his darkness.

"I have time enough for all of you now," it said, and left the children sprawled on the cobblestones as it came for Nicholas.

The yellow king stalked slowly across the courtyard towards him, stamping stone into shards and dust, the magnitude of his pleasure evidenced by the very leisurely tide of his approach. Nicholas wrenched himself up onto an elbow,

A SKULK OF FOXES

spat defiance as he tried to get used to the thought of being dead in the very near future..

"My daughter will do for you," he promised quietly.

"I think not," said the king. He swept one arm in the ragged flutters of his robes and sent Ysa and Yana tumbling across the cobblestones...

―◈―

"...I can't find them!" shouted Thomas from the kitchen. "Di says they're not in the cellar!"

Alain and Andrew were frantic on the second floor, having been through the music room and all the second-floor bedrooms. They converged on the landing with Alexandra and Frederick as Tom and Diana thundered up the stairs.

"Not in the garrets either," said Wyndham the Elder, "but your linen throw over the painting is turned back. I know I was there, Brandy, but it's not like any painting I've ever seen before."

Brandywine paled. "They've gone through," she whispered. "Please no but they've gone through...I can feel it..."

En masse they charged up the stairs at the end of the hallway, turned on the landing and confronted *the painting*...

Something that now bore resemblance to a courtyard in the Old City—as it might be viewed through an open doorway impossibly framed in a forest—surrounded by apple trees inhabited by dozens of cats, afternoon sunlight streaking through the odd shadows made by the towers of the New City...pulsing with the light...beckoning with a voiceless promise. Brandy turned to everyone behind her...

"I'm going," she said, and trembled as she flung herself at the canvas... disappeared into it...

...Sprawled on cobblestones, scraping her knees into blood...already on her feet with the twins a dozen paces away and Windy on the far side of the courtyard with one of his legs twisted in all the wrong directions. She caught up the children, flung them backward into what she prayed were the arms of everyone who had followed her and plunged forward across the courtyard...her eyes locked with Windy's...blurred with terror and tears she stumbled forward in the wake of the tattered yellow monster going for her husband...two vixens rolling across the cobblestones...she clutched at anything along the way that would serve as a weapon and grasped a long splinter of the staff Nicholas had brought with him from somewhere else in the nightmare that had enfolded them. She shrilled defiance...met an unseen smile of utter delight as it turned and caught sight of her... threw herself at it...into it... felt the jagged splinter of a tree long dead and unable to die as it slipped through the yellow rags...heard the thing howl...landed amidst the insult of its ragged robes and found herself crawling...heedless of her knees and anything else in the world...into Windy's arms...

He said, "I think we're okay for now, Branny..." and went blank for a moment from pain. ..woke up as his parents, Tom and Diana, Alain and Andrew and the twins knelt beside Brandywine, with the vixens sniffing distastefully at the corpse of the yellow king.

"I can't move much," he said.

They looked back at tatters turning brown with rot and then into dust.

A SKULK OF FOXES

Brandy asked, "Are we gonna die now?"

Nicholas laughed through the pain, and said "Not quite so surely as a minute ago."

Jamie said, "What *was* that thing?"

Stella said, "We're just kids. Don't mess with us. What's gonna happen now?"

Nicholas looked at the shimmering thing in the middle of the courtyard.

"I think if you can get me back through that we might be okay."

"It's gonna hurt, though...right...?"

Nicholas...approaching delirious, nodded. "Oh yeah...but me not you..." He closed his eyes and said, "I couldn't find 'Rissa or 'Bella or Gareth..."

Stella said, "I don't like this magic stuff all that much."

Jamie just put his head down.

"I tried t'tell it wasn't fun, Stella."

"Let's be careful with Uncle Nicky, okay?" Brandy said.

Nicholas was unconscous as Tom gently lifted him up to where everyone else could support his leg. They nodded and began a slow progress back to the gate Brandywine had created in the middle of the courtyard.

The two vixens watched them until they were gone through, twitched their tails at each other and went to find Kerissa and Arabella.

Chapter Twenty Two – Kerissa Comes to the Castle

With Khalid trotting along unconcernedly beside her, Kerissa allowed herself the luxury of optimism, casting off memories of the unsettling experiences that had been Linden Faire. The landscape grew no friendlier, but to her it felt that having in all likelihood finally discovered the whereabouts of where she was supposed to be going, the last trek to actually get there seemed less harsh. The prospect of re-uniting with Arabella or her father in Qaraq-al-Ossa gave her hope for success in rescuing her mother.

"...After all," she said aloud, "an awful lot of this alternate world stuff hasn't even been real...almost make-believe...things happening that didn't really happen or never will happen unless you end up where it's going on by going through the proper gate... which you don't wanna do anyway, because why get yourself into something nasty when you don't have to...?"

Khalid had a thought that hadn't occurred to her.

Sometimes they are not nasty things? he inquired gently. *Sometimes the nasty things are the ones behind you and the gate is for a good place...?*

Kerissa took a minute or two to mull over that one.

"I suppose that could be true," she said, and gave him a look that held just as much admiration as exasperation, "but

A SKULK OF FOXES

right now I think I'm gonna stick with bein' cranky over this place; that way I'm not gonna be surprised by somethin' I'm not expecting....and even if everything back in the real world isn't all sunshine and rosiness, at least I get t'feel like we're all going back t'stuff we know how t'deal with."

Khalid, being perhaps the most philosophical of his own immediate family, smiled inwardly and picked up the pace, swishing his tail back and forth with his nose up in the air searching for something for which he could make more positive observations. In consequence, he didn't see the chasm that opened soundlessly before them, and would have plunged downward into the tear in the earth's surface if not for Kerissa's quick hand on the scruff of his neck, hauling him back from the abyss. What came for them from out of the ragged tear in the ground was not pretty. Khalid became a wreath round 'Rissa's neck...

It roiled upwards, convulsed all along the edge of the chasm, blind eyes staring into nowhere, scaled and immense with a tongue darting in and out, questing for the scent of living flesh to devour. Somehow that hunger made Kerissa cringe in upon herself, close her eyes, made her desperate to conceal her nakedness, to the exclusion of any other emotion. Khalid nipped her ear...whispered urgently in her head...

More than a little girl, you he said. *Can be helping now, me...*

She opened her eyes as the massive jaws came at them, and with the Khalid's urging lifted her left hand, willed the light of the moonstone on her forefinger into its unseeing eyes and heard it scream, black fluid pouring from its nostrils as its blind eyes exploded and it battered the margin of the crevasse at their feet into clouds of dust and cinders. It lay its length before them, writhing itself into the ground before it finally stopped moving, and its corpse began to smoulder and raise up a stench that sent them running back the way they had come.

"I thought you couldn't do that," she said, not ungratefully, because what had risen up from the earth had scared the daylights out of her. Khalid took his own good long time getting over being scared .

Now we *can* he said, with the beginnings of a cautious smile..

"Bloody good for us," said Kerissa. "That was no fun at all..."

No fun. Bloody good for us echoed Khalid.

―――❦―――

So they continued. As they retraced their steps back to the edge of the chasm, the remains of the *thing* made their eyes water. Kerissa looked in either direction, trying to decide which way they should go around it, but also aware that the tear in the earth had only grown longer, and crossing over it, as she knew they must do, was becoming more and more of an impossibility with every passing moment. Everything around them seemed to be coming apart, distant mountains exploding into fountains of molten rock, the earth splitting open in plumes of noxious gas and geysers of boiling water. She heard Khalid smiling again, in answer to to her thoughts.

"We can do that now...?"

Of course. Doing the river by yourself, but now are we stronger. Now are having more magick...you and *me...*

"What do I do?"

We must be on the other side...the light shows your way...

A SKULK OF FOXES

Her right hand went up to where he had curled around her neck; her left hand she stretched out before them, thinking/willing them to be on the far side of the fissure in the earth, and found them there in half a heartbeat.

"Wow," she said. "Is that all it takes?"

Khalid grinned into her ear.

Is seeming to be...yes?.

"I don't know if we're taking too long, Khalid," she said. "Now that we can, wouldn't it be better t'be there...waiting if we have to...?"

We can go he said, nodding against her cheek.

Kerissa looked into the glowing stone on her finger and willed them to be where they needed to be...recognised what could have been the decorative wrought-iron fencing that surrounded the Amaranth Palace if it had not been scourged into grotesque scrollwork by unimaginable heat.

"Here we are...I think..." she said, and tentatively lifted the latch that secured the wrough-iron gate before them. "I guess I really don't have t'do this anymore...just thinking about being on the other side of it should be enough."

She looked down at her feet but Khalid was still outside rather than inside beside her. He wriggled his way through near to the bottom, and they turned to take their first clear look at the object of their quest—Qaraq-al-Ossa.

At first glance, Kerissa thought, as with just about everything they had encountered thus far, that it bore some resemblance to its counterpart, the Amaranth Palace, but seen slightly out of focus, or under mud-clogged moving water. The stones appeared to be almost fluid themselves, imperceptibly swelling and contracting as if it were a living organism, taking in breath and slowly letting it out again. She felt slightly nauseous watching it, and felt a similar sense of dismay in the dog-fox at her feet...and then one or another of the stones would burst open, spewing a shower of foul-smelling liquid over the ground at their foundation, momentarily exposing a white skeletal structure at its heart before the wound closed in upon itself.

"That sort of answers one question, anyway," she said. "I wonder if this whole thing isn't really what it looks like at all...just something strange and pretty awful pretending to be a castle."

Khalid made no reply, but went carefully before her, sniffing them a path across the sere waste pretending to be a broad pastoral setting for a pretend castle. As they came closer, they could hear the ground sizzling where its "blood" had been spilled, leaving deep furrows in the earth that became populated with pale ribbon-like creatures that writhed and squirmed up into the wan light to lap at it.

Unlike the Amaranth Palace, where a shaded walk led directly to the arcade sheltering the entrance, 'Rissa and Khalid found no obvious means of getting inside the place, and, making certain to be out of range of bleeding stones, began to walk round it in search of a door. Again, Kerissa thought all she need do was wish herself and the fox inside, yet felt reluctanct to do so, not knowing what awaited them. She had spent enough time visiting with Arabella to have a general idea of what the interior of the Amaranth Palace was like, but preferred to go cautiously now, always cognisant of how in Caracosh, not everything was a mirror or corollary of what she had known. At length, halfway round the perimeter of the grounds, they found a small door. Khalid vanished, reappeared a moment later.

Is mostly safe on the other side of this door...only a passage...empty it is seeming...

Kerissa nodded, gathered him up and magicked them past it.

Chapter Twenty Three - Amid the Bones of the Bone Castle

Sebastian lay stunned with surprise, bathed in pale light from the windows flanking Evrard's bed. For a moment he turned, curious to see where Evrard had gone to, and demand an explanation of sorts, but there was no one besides himself in the bedchamber.

He called out softly, received no reply. Waited and called again with the same lack of response. He crawled out of bed and saw clots of earth and tiny scraps of cloth—a sickening yellow in colour—scattered across the rugs that covered the stone floor, and began to feel a dire sense of *normal* having gone utterly wrong. He dressed quickly and dashed into the corridors of the wing that housed Evrard's living quarters, shouting for

servants and guardsmen, cursing himself for letting Evrard isolate them for the night, and trembling with the knowledge that *he* was responsible for whatever had occurred.

Edmund and Annie Branny are gonna have my head he thought, trying to stifle panic and start thinking constructively.

When the first rush of palace staff turned toward him from the far end of the corridor leading back into the day-to-day environs of the palace, he turned them round at once.

A SKULK OF FOXES

"The king's disappeared!" he cried. "Someone's taken him I don't know how just seal the grounds make certain *no one* leaves the palace!"

Moments later he was alone again, left with only the echoes of footfalls and voices receding along the passage that crossed the corridor. He stood in light filtered down through an intricacy of mirrored conduits running down from skylights on the roof. The palace had been wired for the new electrical lamps, but they were used only on days when the skies over the City remained overcast, and during the night. Sebastian leaned against an arras-ed wall and took stock of the situation, intuitively linking his friend's disappearnce with the events and revelations he'd been party to in St John's Mews a few days earlier.

As he stood there alone, he felt a sudden tremor of the stone beneath his feet, a brief moment when it seemed his eyes had gone blurry and the corridor to either side of him had *moved*—in an earthquake-wise fashion—before righting itself. He thought to hear one last fading echo of sound from those he had charged to seal the palace grounds, but recognised the sound as an impossibility of coming from Evrard's staff...something from somewhere else...dying. He walked back into Evrard's bedchamber and retrieved weaponry, knowing full well they would serve him not at all but feeling better about it anyway, and felt the palace shift and shudder beneath his feet again.

"This has got t'be part and parcel of the girls and Nicholas wandering off t'wherever t'save Gareth," he said to no one. "I need t'figure out where Ev fits into this...how taking *him* relates t'them..."

He realised he had no way of knowing, only that everything his family had worked for over twenty years had been put at risk if Evrard de Montigny...*de Montenay*...were taken from the throne of the realm...

"It's them again," he thought aloud. "Somehow I *know* it's them all over again..."

He didn't need to tell himself who qualified as *them*. In the place where he lived within the safety and unyielding bonds of family, he *knew*...

"For all the good it's gonna do me now," he said, and went to join the rest of those in the Amaranth Palace gone in search of their king.

"Here we are...again," said Kerissa, shivering, suddenly chilled for lack of clothing and mildly terrified by the empty passage before her and Khalid.

The stone walls felt like they were contracting inward to bury her—the intruder with her bare back pressed against what only looked like an iron-hinged oaken door—like fingers curling into places she'd never allowed anyone to go but 'Bella. She lifted her left hand begging the moonstone for light...something...to dispel the sense of being violated...closed her eyes against tears, knowing that now they had no time for her fear. The floor at her feet convulsed, pitching her and Khalid against one of the walls, and she recoiled in disgust as the "fingers" again crept into her sense of self...made her tremble with desire that was an absolute screaming of despair and revulsion... and a thought of never ever again having her girl back...

A SKULK OF FOXES

"Oh 'Bella..." she whimpered, sinking to her knees. "What have we done? Why's this happening please make it stop I know I'm supposed t'be the one looking after you but I don't know how t'do it anymore."

In answer the floor before her shimmered, and Khalid leapt from her shoulders to rub noses with his sisters.

Ysa said *The undying one who ruled this land is dead, Kerissa Davies. Your Brandywine did this, in defense of the children and the one you call Windy. Now we must hurry, else we are trapped here when Caracosh begins to come apart...*

Kerissa leaned forward to embrace them all, struggled to her feet wiping tears from her face.

"I still don't know where I'm supposed t'be here or what I'm supposed t'do..."

We must go down, Kerissa Davies said Yana. *Now there is only down for us going...*

"Is 'Bella here? Can we find her first?"

Arabella can be wherever she chooses said Ysa *She must find us...*

"So we're going...now...all three of us...?"

Windy is safe. The children are safe...

"So it's still up t'you and me and 'Bella...here...t'find my da and my mum..."

Three foxy faces nodded up at her.

Is... they said in unison. *Also Hasan...*

She could sense that something had been radically altered in the fabric of the place she had come to. She had no way of knowing that her own mother had managed what an eternity of Time had been unable to do; that its source had been a simple act of something that did not seem to exist in Caracosh, if it had ever existed there at all, and so she looked back at the ridgetop where she had waved a goodbye to the round little priest and then determined that she knew all she needed to know, and with that prescience of knowing was come to her the urgency that had been shrouded by the *glamourie* of those who still would have the vast measure of their hatred turned upon her family.

We can't be trapped here when it comes apart she told herself. *I gotta find 'Rissa and we've gotta find her mum and her da and be gone...soon...*

She closed her eyes, conjured in her mind the nightmare castle with its walls of living stone that creaked and groaned and ground itself upon its own bones, and hemorrhaged whatever it was that flowed past them and gave them sentience, and she screamed frustration...lifted a hand and shattered a score of realities to reach the one she sought.

I'm coming, 'Rissa she promised. *This has gone on long enough...*

Sebastian raced the length and breadth of the Amaranth Palace, encountered search parties and servitors gone frantic with the same sense of urgency that now had him running wide-eyed and heedless into every corner he could find that might give him a clue about where to find Evrard. At length he came to the audience hall, where nearly everyone in the palace had gathered...finally...after hours of searching...to stand with nothing to show for their efforts.

A SKULK OF FOXES

"Nothing," said the captain of the guard. "He's not here. How did you know? Why did you call us?"

"I was with him!" cried Sebastian. "One moment we were there...together...and then he was gone. You can't have searched everywhere. He *must* be here..."

"We've *been* everywhere," said the captain of the guard impatiently, taking some small offense at Sebastian's intimation that he had not done his part. "You have no right or station to question me in that way."

"He's my king as well as my friend!"

"Perhaps not so much as you would have us believe. The realm has only just survived the Antillians. Perhaps you know *them* still, and better than you would have us know..."

"He must be here. We've not been into every corner...every cupboard..."

"There are only the dungeons, that Evrard himself commanded the door leading down to them be sealed with stone and mortar."

"Then open it up again, dammit! If the king's nowhere t'be found on this side of that door, then he must be on other..."

<hr>

The corridors began a slow but steady increase in the intensity of the tremors that rose up from beneath them. Paving stones beneath their feet would crack, grind themselves into powder to fill the surge of vein-like fissures and then gape wide under their feet. The walls would swell and bulge as if filling with fluid, then split wide open as she had seen them do outside the walls of the castle, flooding the passageway, making progress throughly distasteful enough that all three foxes found shelter on her shoulders and she closed her eyes to gingerly do a dance through the swill. Ysa whispered:

Yana will stay. Khalid and I will go to find those we must find...

In their usual fashion, the two eldest did an instant disappear and Kerissa was left to deal with the youngest as her only companion. She became aware of a wee foxy nose beside one ear, wrinkling up in response to the stench around them, smiled in spite of the fact that whatever she was wading through to the tops of her toes did indeed stink like all get-out.

"When this is over I'm gonna take a bath for a month," she said bitterly.

Yana laughed in such wise as foxes laughed, then sunk her claws into Kerissa's shoulder as the paving stones shuddered beneath them, tossed them to one wall of the passage and then against the other. Kerissa went into a panic as that side of the passage felt like it had dissolved as she came in contact with it, yet when the tremors stopped, it seemed as if they still were where they had been.

Not the same said Yana. *Is looking like, but not...*

"So we're in the Bone Castle...but a different one than the one we walked into...?"

Yana nodded yes.

Kerissa said, "Lovely...and look at all this nasty stuff on my feet...!"

The corridor plunged downward...a score of slimed steps going further down into the dark. When they reached the bottom of them, she found the walls had come alight with phosphorescence, a pale unwavering light thoroughy unlike that of her moonstone, conducive to what Jamie once had

A SKULK OF FOXES

called "tossing cookies", though at the time no one knew what on earth he was talking about..

Kerissa stopped...looked at her surroundings, that had been nothing but the essence of Care and Woe for as long as she could keep her mind from throwing up metaphorical hands and fleeing into the arms of Despair. She realised she was crying again...called out for her mother and father and Arabella and everything that was nothing like where she was now. Her knees went into the nasty stuff. Yana was concerned. Somewhere nearby, someone called out to them...

Ysa and Khalid materialised somewhere else and went about in the gloom and the sludge with their nostrils twitching and their eyes crossing as they moved about in the castle's bones. They had no need of conversation; their thoughts were instantly one and the same between them, so they went about in the gloom and the slime and marvelled at what humankind had fashioned out of the fabric of the universe.

The corridors of stone shuddered beneath their paws; some came apart beneath them and spurted out a foul mockery of lifeblood. Leaping aside they would look back over their shoulders and see the splintered bones of the castle thrusting themselves up into the murk, like living things waiting to be healed in a place where Life only came to die.

Alone and on their own they could go anywhere they pleased, no longer weighed down by the souls and hopes of human things. They explored the last outpost...the heart of Caracosh... even as it began to come apart beneath them.

That was how they came to the last door...the last gate...the one hidden beneath every last Hope and Dream, the one that led into the *in-between*...

From a distance they deemed to be safe, they stared into it briefly, knew better than to even nose at it lest it draw them in and never let them go. Then they turned, trotted up the highway from Hell and never looked back.

Evrard had heard a familiar voice, the sound of someone a lifetime away...in pain...far and away above him as he lay on the cold dank stones of his prison. The thing in yellow had been gone for...he had no way of knowing for how long...yet in its absence he had tried to muster up a sense of optimism that for all the strangeness had taken him from Sebastian beside him in his bed, there might...must be...an equal if not greater strange to rescue him, bring him out from what he *knew* was a place he was never meant to survive.

He roused himself up from where he lay curled upon a bed of rags in the corner of the dungeon and began to shout as if his life depended on it...and knowing likely it did...

She went now in something akin to fury, no longer giving care to who or what she encountered as she staggered from one time-stream to the next, shadow-sword and shadow-dagger drawn, slashing away at anything crossing her path that was unknown to her. She could feel the bones of the castle grinding together, feel their insensate agony, feel them coming apart,

A SKULK OF FOXES

tearing themselves loose one from the next as Caracosh died beneath her feet. If not for the ones she had sworn to herself to save, she would have joined them in death-song...happily...knowing full well that there would be no end for her...

She told herself, "Just be quiet and do your job, Arabella...just be quiet and do your job..."

Kerissa felt Yana's tongue on her face, lapping gently at her tears, heard some sort of soothing fox-whisper in her head telling her not to be sad, that it was only the way things worked in Caracosh. She nodded, scrubbed at her face with both hands and got back on her feet, shaking her head, again feeling thoroughly put-out by the "nasty stuff" that now spattered her all the way up past her knees.

"You're right I know, Yana. It's just that it feels like we've been at this forever and I don't remember sleeping at all. I guess I'm just tired..."

Yana nodded.

Tired, yes....but listen...!

Now there was an urgency in the vixen's tone. Kerissa stilled her breathing, listened to her heart beating widly for a moment before she took a deep breaths to still it as well. Then she heard the voice...calling from somewhere in the darkness beyond the reach of her ring's light.

"Where are you?" she cried. "Who are you?"

Stone that should have echoed to the sound of her voice swallowed it instead, yet she heard a reply...recognised *Evrard*...before it too faded into the maelstrom agony of a time-stream dying. She ran down the corridor with Yana clinging to her neck, high-stepping through the muck as the walls again began to shudder and grind themselves into the ooze at her feet.

"Evrard it's 'Rissa keep shouting I'll find you...!"

The passageway became a living thing that tossed beneath her feet, twisted away from her every time she sought to steady herself against the walls. Evrard's voice became a constant call to her, leading her deeper into the earth with the darkness fleeing ahead of her in the light cast forward by her ring. The stone now paled, seemed to become something porous...brittle...almost translucent...crumbling down around her with the ceiling coming apart over her head, dropping lower and lower with her every step.

He is not here! said Yana.

"Yana I can hear him!"

Not in this time/place, him...you must go to another for finding him...

Kerissa swore under her breath, stopped dead in the middle of a pool of muck and looked to either side for some indication of where they could go. The ceiling of the passage behind her collapsed. She shuddered, closed her eyes, flung her left hand outward into the wall beside her and felt her skin being scraped by castle-bones even as it sucked her through into another passage.

She called to Evrard again. Heard him reply, closer now. Flung them through another wall. And a third. Found themselves with their backs against bricks rather than stone.

Is here said Yana. *Down more, but here...*

Gratefully, Kerissa raced down a passage that still bore resemblance to a place not quite ready to come apart in the

A SKULK OF FOXES

slow disintegration of everything else around them. She called to Evrard after every half score of strides, leaned leftwards into yet another downward plunge of corridor and a hundred yards along slid to a stop beside a massive door hinged and bolted in black iron.

"Evrard?

"'Rissa is that really you?"

"It is," she said. "What on earth are you doing down here?"

"I'm taking a holiday, 'Rissa," came his impatient reply.

"No need t'be huffy. What's *down here*, anyway...?"

"An old dungeon in the Amaranth Palace. Or one that resembles it, at any rate."

"You decided t'take a holiday in an old dungeon."

"'Rissa don't be a wise-ass can you get me out of here?"

"I can try," she said.

"Please do," he said. "Anytime in the next ten seconds would be lovely."

"He's awfully cute, y'know," she said to Yana. "And he gets all red if you tease him."

"What's that?" asked Evrard.

"Nothing," she said, smiling for the first time in what felt like forever. She asked Yana *Can you help?* and received a nod beside her ear in the same instant they simply stepped through the oaken door and found Evrard on the other side.

"You've not got any clothes on!" said Kerissa. "Who holidays in places like this without any clothing?"

Evrard wondered at the soft glow of light on her hand, the fox round her shoulders, and then did very little to disguise his own curiosity as to why *she* wasn't wearing any clothing.

"*I'm* not on holiday," she sniffed, and then: "We gotta get out of here in a hurry though, Evrard. There's all sorts of stuff goin' on, most of it wonkier than either one of us wants t'deal with..."

"There's this nasty thing in yellow rags.." he said.

Kerissa shook her head.

"Not anymore. Annie Branny killed him."

"Annie Brandy killed him? Brandywine? Arabella's mom?"

Kerissa nodded.

"Yep. She opened a gate and showed up in time t'save Uncle Windy and the twins."

"I have no idea what any of that means, Kerissa. Arabella's mother opened a *gate*...and then killed the thing that kidnapped *me*...?"

"I said so, didn't I?...and it doesn't matter if you don't understand just now, Evrard. Come give us a hug and we'll see if we can be somewhere else where I can explain..."

Suddenly Kerissa was feeling more like herself. Evrard didn't require a second invitation.

Another time-stream shattered round her to fall at her feet like broken glass. The passageway was dank and dark with no light whatsoever to be seen, but Arabella could see her surroundings quite well in despite. Had anyone been nearby to observe her in darkness, they would have found her slumped against a wall with her eyes closed, exhausted, sword and dagger drawn but scraping in shadow-fashion against the stone floor as she slid down the wall, shivered at the cold and wet against the back of her thighs.

A SKULK OF FOXES

The constant groan and splintering of the stone around her became louder and louder, scattering her thoughts in five directions every time she tried to collect them, decide what to do next. Eventually she dragged herself back onto her feet and stumbled along the corridor, found herself at the intersection of one more wide than the one she had left behind her, this one leading upward, and another to her right going down again. In the end it was easier to simply continue going forward, until she came to a small open chamber with three other corridors converging upon it, a place she was certain she'd seen before...

The lower levels of the Palace... she thought. *Me and 'Rissa got lost down here once...so I must be leaving the dungeons behind me...*

It had been on one of her mother's many visits to the Palace in her *role* as the Second Assistant to the Royal Stationer, when they'd grown tired of amusing themselves in places they'd already been to on many other occasions. Kerissa had been reluctant, but then had gotten caught up in her little sister's sense of adventure. Four hours later they had been in this very chamber, trying to make a choice about which way to go in order to get back; gratefully, they'd heard footsteps and started shouting and laughing for someone to come save them. This time the footsteps were unheard, though the face in torchlight that appeared out of one of the other corridors was much more familiar to her than the unnamed servitor who had found them as children. He stopped abruptly, and scowled, but then the elegant bearded face softened into a delighted smile.

"Well...finally..." said Renard de Montenay. "I've been waiting for you, but never for a moment believed you could make your way here."

"I'm full of wonderful surprises," replied Arabella, "like the five I put into your back as you *ran away* from two girls..."

She took a step away from him, felt the stone cold against her back as he moved to a place in centre of the chamber, made a great show of drawing a longsword from his belt, his black-as-night eyes never leaving hers, glistening with anticipation.

"Perhaps you feel a sense of accomplishment at having killed an unarmed man," he suggested.

"Perhaps if my horse had not gotten between you and us, you'd have had a better time killing us in our sleep....brave soul that *you* are..."

Arabella was pleased to see that Renard de Montenay still reacted poorly—and predictably—to mockery from others. His hand twitched on the hilt of his sword and the scowl returned to his face.

"Where is your *afrique*, child?

"You mean my sister Kerissa? Oh she wanted to come along...on the off chance we might meet up with you again, but I told her she needn't waste any of her time or effort, that I could deal with you quite well enough on my own."

De Montenay's face darkened with a surge of anger, as Arabella had intended it should, and she saw veins standing out in his forehead and throat as he fought back on his rage.

"Having died once at my hands, I was hoping you'd have the good sense to stay away from me...but I see that Death has not improved your disposition at all. It's a shame, because now I have t'kill you all over again..."

A SKULK OF FOXES

De Montenay ground his teeth to echo the dissolution of the Bone Castle around them. He took a step forward as Arabella raised her sword.

"Stupid girl...your steel is of no use here.."

Arabella grinned. "That's why I left my sword and daggers behind...*after* I'd made shadows of them."

De Montenay stopped, an inkling of dismay showing on his face. Arabella went on taunting him, knowing full well that every ounce of hatred and rage she could foster in him could only serve to her advantage,

"D'you remember Evrard...the son you tried t'murder in Swinton...? He sits on the Amaranth Throne now, the throne you thought belonged t'you. It was my mom who put him there. You *must* remember her...I think you once called her a street-whore. Not bad work for so lowly a creature, wouldn't you say?"

"This time I'm going to make certain you die slowly," he snarled.

Arabella smiled again.

"Too late. You missed a lot of stuff, Renard," she said. "You missed my father and the mother of my *afrique* totally destroy the Antillian fleet. You missed my aunt and uncle's boys destroy their ground army before they even got off the beach west of the City. And you missed how I put a real steel dagger into the brain of your precious sorcerer."

"You're lying, of course," said de Montenay, "and I *will* kill you.".

Arabella shrugged. "I forgot t'tell that I died in the process of killing the sorcerer; that my *afrique's* mother brought me back, so killing me is gonna take a lot more doing than you think."

"That's impossible!"

"Yet here we are...old friends re-united..." said Arabella. "And even if everything I've said is a lie and the two of us are here just because we've somehow ended up here for whatever reason, you still don't get t'kill me."

"You think not."

"I don't have t'think anything, Renard. I'm just better than you. You're bigger and stronger and I'm *just a girl*...but I can beat you with my eyes closed."

De Montenay roared, all his patience gone as he raised his sword up and came at her, flinging his torch against the wall.

"Don't let that go out, Renard," she cautioned him. "If I close my eyes I don't need the light, but you...well...you're gonna need all the help you can get..."

And then Arabella closed her eyes and parried his two-handed overhead attack, flung the blade sideways and drove the point of her dueling sword into the soft flesh where de Montenay's ribs dipped down to his hip on his left side.

He staggered backwards, looked briefly down at the blood welling out from his tunic and leapt at her again. This time he thrust at her from below, lunging forward; she turned sideways, stepped past his outthrust arm and put her dagger into the fleshy part of his thigh before kicking the leg out from under him. She opened her eyes, shook her head in mock sorrow.

"I'm just a girl, Renard," she said. As he staggered back onto his feet she saw doubt and fear in his eyes. "Just a girl," she whispered, and closed her eyes again.

A SKULK OF FOXES

For a time they danced in the flickering torchlight, Arabella never anywhere near the point or edge of de Montenay's greatsword. At times he might close with her, but then only to receive another thrust of her dagger somewhere, to bleed him, cause him pain, but allow him to continue nevertheless. Occasionally she would open her eyes so he could see the imminence of the last moments of the second "life" that had been granted to him.

"You'd not even be here if Zoraya had not tried t'be kind," she whispered into his ear, and slipped her dagger up into the heavy muscles of his back behind his sword arm.

"You'd not be anything...just dust...the empty lifeless dust of a life wasted in cruelty..."

The hand that held de Montenay's sword went numb and it fell to the floor as he staggered backwards against a far wall, sank slowly to his knees. Arabella came to stand over him, and he saw tears falling from her eyes...still closed...

"I'm sure you've got nothing of value t'say," she sobbed, and put the point of her sword into his throat.

***

She willed them past the bricks and mortar at the head of the passage that led downward into the old dungeons of the Amaranth Palace, arms round each other's waists as they climbed up the stone paves and...somewhere...could hear the place coming apart around them, though in their time-stream everything appeared to be as much of the Amaranth Palace as they were accustomed to. Yana seemed happy...grinned and swatted Evrard with her tail whenever she caught him eyeing her sideways.

MICHAEL SUMMERLEIGH

Not speaking to this one yet she said to Kerissa.

Good idea she replied. *He's had more than enough puzzlement for today...*

At length, beyond the glow of Kerissa's ring, they saw a flickering of light ahead of them and without conscious thought increased their pace together. The passageway widened a bit and they found themselves in a small circular chamber where three other corridors converged, and on the far side something ...someone...they both knew... standing over the collapsed body of someone equally familiar for entirely different reasons.

" 'Bella...'Bella is that you...?"

Kerissa let go of Evrard and rushed forward as Arabella turned to them, stopped halfway across the chamber in shock...

"'Bella...?"

She could not describe what it was that brought her up short...kept her from falling into the arms of the girl who stood over a corpse with both a shadow-sword and dagger bloodied in her hands.

"It's me, 'Rissa. I'm sorry I went without you."

Whatever it was, for a moment it fell away from her beloved girl, and Arabella stood there, shivering, her weapons falling to the stones at her feet.

'It's almost over, 'Rissa. I promise. You have t'go. You can't stay here. I'm losing track of where we are...you have t'get back to the courtyard...find the Mews..."

"Your mom made a gate...a door..."

Arabella nodded. "I know. Hello, Evrard. You should go with Kerissa, okay?"

He looked past her.

A SKULK OF FOXES

"Is that my father?"

She nodded.

"I killed him again."

Evrard continued to stare at the corpse against the wall...watched it slowly fade away until there was nothing but a thin layer of dust to cloud the stones.

"You guys don't have any clothes," said Arabella. "Aren't you cold? Let me make you warm, okay..."

She reached for them, drew them into her arms and put her head down between them, looked up long enough to whisper...

Hello Yana...

...Before she conjured heat up and around and into the two in her arms.

There was a shimmer beside them, and two more foxes materialised out of nowhere as shouts and footfalls echoed from another of the passages that opened onto the chamber.

At the head of a crowd of palace staff, Sebastian came to a standstill, wide-eyed and unsure of where to look or what to say. Arabella looked up at him.

"Hello, Sebastian," she said. "You don't have t'be frantic anymore. 'Rissa and the foxes can magick you and Evrard wherever you wanna go..."

"No!" cried Kerissa. "I'm going with you, 'Bella, I won't let you go without me..."

"You can't, 'Rissa. I'm the only one can get t'where your mum and da are now...bring them out together..."

Arabella stepped back from them, watched tears well up in Kerissa's beautiful eyes as Sebastian stripped off his shirt, draped it over her and eased her arms into the sleeves.

"Please don't go...don't leave me again I can't bear it..."

"I promise I'll come back, baby...a lot faster this time...I promise...I swear..."

She looked at Sebastian, and Evrard only just beginning to be uncomfortable now he was the only one completely naked.

"Somehow we seem t'be wandering in and out of our own time-stream, that you found us here at all. Ev..rard... our king...looks like he'd be grateful if somebody would take him back up into the palace and find him some trousers...but I think you gotta do it fast..."

Sebastian looked doubtful.

"I'm gonna fix it, Sebastian. Go on...please..me and 'Rissa need a few minutes..."

When they we were gone she turned and put her head on Kerissa's shoulder, her arms round her tight enough they both needed to draw breath back into their lungs she whispered:

"If you come with, 'Rissa, you'll never be able to come back here...into this life. You and me and your mum and da will have to...I dunno...live?...on this side, away from the life we wanted before all of this began.

"You have t'trust me, baby, let me go one more time so all the bad stuff can finally stop.

"Please, go back t'the Mews, take these furry loons with you and tell everyone there that I'll be along as soon as I can..."

"'Bella..."

"No 'Rissa you *have* t'do what I say. You *have* t'let me go by myself..."

Arabella closed her eyes, unable to bear the stricken look she knew was on Kerissa's face, as if wanting her to be safely home with their family around her was in some way a rebuke, a denial of the unshakable thing between them.

A SKULK OF FOXES

"Please, 'Rissa...I'm begging you...I can manage okay this once I just want you t'be safe again..."

She looked down at three fox faces staring up at the pair of them, *spoke* a request that launched them up into Kerissa's arms and over her shoulders. When they had spirited her away, she turned, retrieved her weapons...stepped out of the Amaranth Palace and started down the corridor to the bottom of the Bone Castle...

Chapter Twenty Five – Sorcerer's End

From the moment she stepped out of her own continuum, she was surrounded again by the slow thundering collapse of the one that housed Qaraq-al-Ossa. The corridors she now traversed came apart under her feet...spewed filth and fragments of bone in her wake and in her path, skulls shattering against walls shattering against themselves and narrow passageways gaping wide into vast dizzying panoramas of disaster.

She sensed that with the end of the yellow king in Caracosh, a thread that had held a great portion of one corner of the universe together had become unravelled; that when it was gone, forces greater even than the Magick would again hold sway in the vacuum left by their demise. She had no desire to be there when it happened, test herself against forces so devoid of any consideration or relevance to sentient living things. She reared up on her toes and raced forward, headlong into the maelstrom sucking Caracosh into oblivion.

The corridor lost all semblance of belonging to even a relative construct of the Amaranth Palace. Everything fell away...dissolved around her...she found herself at a standstill, standing on nothingness, with no up or down or sideways, the path she sought now but a heartbeat away...a leap across the

A SKULK OF FOXES

Void...into the Void Beyond...that came alive in front of her in the confluence of a thousand continua at once...exploding outward... raining down around her in a deafening fireworks display of destructon....

The sorcerer floated serenely in the centre of it all, smiling his razour-toothed smile, the arcane stitchery of his embroidered robes moving in cosmic wind.

I have not forgotten you.

Arabella frowned.

"You've not come at a very good time," she said peevishly.

My apologies. I thought you might welcome a distracton...an excuse not to go...there...

He cast a quick glance over his shoulder at the coruscation of darkness behind him.

It's a dreadful place, you know. It's where those who are truly damned come to know the full measure of their failures and transgressions. It gives me infinite pleasure to know that two of those dear to you—one who has been my enemy for centuries—are suffering there without end.

"All the more reason for me to bring them out, " said Arabella.

You are naïve. Even if you were to win your way past me, that place is more than your poor stupid cow-brain could bear...or the flesh and bone that houses it...

"I killed you once before."

You will not do so again. I made a mistake in allowing you to come so close to me, when I had your precious Zoraya on her knees...

"You didn't make any mistake, Chakidze. That was your arrogance and pride...just like when it allowed Zoraya to imprison you three thousand years ago. You haven't learned anything, and it's your arrogance now t'think you know anything more about me than you knew when we first met each other. *I* know *your* name. "

As I know yours, Arabella Wyndham...

"But that's all you know, because you can't even begin t'understand what I *am*. But I know your name *and* I know what you are. That means I don't have t'be afraid of you.

"I tried t'tell poor old Renard de Montenay that the only reason he could exist again...at all... even here...was because my family loved me more than he...or you...know how to hate."

You betray your fear with so many words, Arabella Wyndham. And your sword will not save you from me.

"I don't need my sword t'save me from you, Chakidze. That's how little you *know* about me..."

She drew it and flung it away, arc-ing it into the aether, and as it sparked into non-existence she saw Doubt begin to creep into the animal eyes, the human-seeming shape begin to waver and change as the robes fell away and human limbs stretched, hands lengthened into claws, the jaw of the sorcerer thrusting outward to expose yellowed fangs gone to rot at their roots. His robes disintegrated and the hyaena hackles that rose up along his spine fluttered and rustled in the wind. He took a step forward, raised up one clawed hand and clenched it round where he willed Arabella's throat to be...

Found nothing in his grasp. Snarled. Arabella smiled, shook her head in mock sadness.

"You got nowhere t'run, *Chakidze*..." she said, drawing out each syllable of his name. "And you know I can't...won't...let you go...that this time will be the last time for you..."

A SKULK OF FOXES

Again, he raised up a hand to take her, claws curling upward to repay her for a dagger-thrust six months old. Again there was nothing but tortured air to meet his grasp. The animal eyes narrowed, grew focused upon her and drew her closer...one step... another...

He howled in conquest, and then staggered backwards as Arabella swept the space between them with a gesture of contempt, stunned him into silence.

"I don't have much more time t'waste on you, Chakidze," she whispered.

The emptiness around them shuddered. The sorcerer straightened himself, strode towards her, towering over her, arms flung outward to crush her, jaws drooling and spewing the stench of something that should have died somewhere in the primordial ooze of pre-history. Arabella leapt forward as she had done once before, but this time thrust her *hand* forward...into his chest...shattering his breastbone...clutching at the heart beating beneath it...tearing it loose and holding it aloft in front of his eyes as a shadow-dagger from her belt drove upward from beneath its chin into its brain.

"I told you I didn't need my sword," she said, and snapped the blade off at the hilt.

Chapter Twenty Six - Arabella In-Between

The animal eyes widened in disbelief as blood coursed down over her hand and his chest. He sagged to his knees, where Arabella could look directly into his eyes, that *now* seemed to understand. There was a moment of bright terror, and then the light in them faded away as he collapsed, fell away into the emptiness surrounding them.

Arabella shook her hand once, watched the scattered blood of the sorcerer evapourate in the aether. She took three long strides and leapt into the blackness beyond where he had been, and even the thought of Kerissa fled from her in that instant, along with everything that she had ever known in her life. The darkness filled itself with the roar of continua that numbered into infinity, the kaleidoscope of the Universe and all things that were part of it, all rushing past her, somehow managing never to collide with each other, going on forever....dying... resurrecting themselves...lives being lived until their end... lives being lived endlessly...

She tried to speak, tried to dampen the immensity and horror with the sound of her own voice, and realised she was no longer even a thread in the fabric of the Everywhere/Everything; that she was moving beyond it, to exist somewhere outside of it, and all that was left for her was to find Gareth and

A SKULK OF FOXES

Zoraya and bring them to a place where in some way *they* could be together again.

The realities streamed past her in every direction, each one prismed by what could have been a clouded pane of window glass. She crashed through one and found herself in another, where a different choice made created yet another reality every bit as valid as the one it had destroyed. She heard her mother say:

"'Bella you musn't blame him sometimes boys are like that..."

Arabella was ten years old and enraged because Edmund had become so angry with her. She couldn't even remember what she'd done...teased him...maybe...made some remark about how she belonged to Kerissa and boys were pretty yucky after all and just because they were all in the same family didn't mean she had to like him at all...

"You're a big moose, Edmund. No one loves a big moose...only other mooses..."

And she had taken a perverse satisfaction in watching him slink away in tears with his head down, all his promises and devotion spurned by the ferocity of her loyalty to Kerissa.

"He loves you, 'Bella," said her mother.

"Well I love 'Rissa so it's stupid for him t'say..."

"'Bella there's all sorts of ways to love the people you love and who love you..."

She cringed at the cruelty of a ten-year old girl who had lived in a different lifeline, and became lost again in the lives rushing past/around/through her in the midst of the roar of the cosmic river until it became silent again as she watched a small blonde girl-child of perhaps four years break into tears and fall at the feet of another, chocolate-skinned and a few years older...

"...'Wissa don't go..."

"...Go away I don't want you anymore," she said. "No one pays any attention to me now. It's always about Arabella...look how beautiful she is...see how smart she is... look at Arabella...look at Arabella...! I'm tired of looking I hate you..."

The dark-skinned girl turned and walked away, never looking back, never acknowledging the anguish of the other...

...As Arabella flung herself through a shimmer of Time and trembled to have witnessed herself reacting to something that in her own memory had never happened... twisted herself away and found herself on the loveseat in the music room of the coach house in St John's Mews...with her father...frowning at her...

"Arabella you can't go on treating her like this," he said. "Zori and Gareth have been here half a dozen times and they say 'Rissa is mad with grief because you won't even speak to her anymore. I'm not trying t'tell you how to live your life, honey, but please don't be cruel. That's not how your mother and I taught you...it's not who you are..."

"Daddy, you don't know! She thinks I belong to her. If I even look at anyone else she gets crazy jealous. Just because you and mom are friends with Gareth and Zori doesn't mean I have t'put up with her trying t'run my life...she's a lunatic, daddy, she needs help so badly..."

...And then stumbling away from yet another part of a life she'd never lived she began to weep, knowing it was not anything she would ever have said or even thought of Kerissa, except in the place she had been it was what had happened, and

A SKULK OF FOXES

she had some horrible inkling of how Kerissa somehow had heard about what she'd said and thrown herself off a bridge, into the Findhorn, and drowned...

"I can't do this anymore," she whispered, but a voice inside her said:

Of course you can....and you will...because it's what you were meant to do...and it's who you are now and nothing you can do or say or think will change what you've become...

Arabella wondered just what it was she had become, smashed through another pane of cosmic glass in search of Zoraya and her uncle Gareth...

...Came to desolation in another desert ...another wasteland of emotion and loss where she wept and begged to be given a life back...untroubled...Kerissa between her legs...day after day of stupid blind *just me and my love*...being wet and endless...

She became so tired of being alone...the interminable search through everywhere to save living things she could barely remember being a part of her life and Love in the middle of the chaos...the never-ending journey towards some kind of peace she couldn't even define...

She cried...whispered...

'Rissa please come save me. I'm so tired...

It was nothing that had never happened before, when the world had become too much for her...more than she had ever wanted to ever want from any of it...

Just take care of me...please...I don't know what t'do....please help me....

But she knew...she knew...that part of her life was over...

There was nothing in it for her except to go on, stumble her her way forward and hope she would be in time...that it wouldn't kill her...that 'Rissa would be there when it was over.

"Oh 'Bella I love you so much..."
"Don't leave me, 'Rissa..."
"Never..."
"I can't live.."
"Baby you have to....you're all the hope we've got..."
"I miss you so much..."
"It's not about us anymore, 'Bella..."
"So why...?"
"Because..."
"That's not a good answer."
"Because somewhere someone has to care...someone needs to love as hard as you. It's the only thing can save us..."
"I'm so scared without you."
"I know, baby, but your heart is bigger than mine...the world needs you..."
"You're the world, 'Rissa..."
"No 'Bella. I'm just...me...dying for you..."
"Don't go....please..."
"'Bella ...our world isn't made of endless choices that we get t'make...even where you are now...don't you see that?"
"But you've always looked after me. What do I do...who's gonna take care of me...?"
"You don't need anyone t'do that anymore, 'Bella. It's just the way things've turned out, y'know...? Some of it's because of the things we did, and some of it's for the things we didn't do..."
"I don't understand any of that, 'Rissa, how am I gonna Iive without you?"

A SKULK OF FOXES

"Remember what you mom always said, baby. I'll see you somewhere... someday..."
"Rissa..."
"G'bye 'Bella. I love you...you're the only one...forever..."

She became frantic for a while, lost track of whatever Time might be in the place she had come to, smashed into and through hundreds of time-streams, too frightened to stop, or pay any attention to the possibility that she might be a force of destruction even greater than that of the ones who had tried to destroy her and her family.

She encountered the lives of total strangers, watched their joys become nightmares, suffered with them through sorrows beyond imagining. There had been two lovers grown so enamoured of *her* that they began to resent each other; a woman whose small dog, that had been her most loyal companion for almost a dozen years, suddenly found its devotion to be intolerable; two brothers who had let a small disagreement blossom into a virulent hatred; a dying patriarch goading his children into competition for a non-existent inheritance.

Her reference points, the ones that in some way had borne resemblance to her own life, slowly faded away into the torrent of broken lives she came upon one after another, until the only way she managed to go on was to block all of it from her active consciousness and fill her thoughts with nothing but images and memories of Kerissa as they had known each other, and the ongoing search to find Gareth gone in search of Zoraya.

MICHAEL SUMMERLEIGH

As she went deeper and deeper into the timestreams in-between she began to realise that whatever influence she might have had on the other side had become weaker and weaker; that she was fast coming to where she could no longer touch, or bring anything to bear upon the existences of those she encountered; that their lives had ceased to be anything more than a never-ending loop of the same tragedies and despair that had sent them to a midnight carnival in a Linden Faire she had never seen, to ride up into the sky and then cast themselves into the Void......

Somewhere along the way, everything stopped being strange and dreadful and she found a corner of the in-between that was dark and dreary, but finally quiet, without the echoing roar and thunder of catastrophic lives rushing by in every direction. The cries and desperate whispers of lives long since denied any hope of salvation slowly grew silent; she moved in a cocoon of her own thoughts and memories and searched for her beloved's parents with eyes that sought only to light upon *them*, seeing little or nothing of anyone or anything else.

The world as she came to know it was fluid—landscapes and settings that drifted in and out of her awareness or ability to relate to them on a physical level. She felt as if she were floating on an unseen tide that drew her ever onward, and with a jolt of pure terror when she recognised the place she had been drawn into as the clifftop outside of Bedford where she and Chakidze had spiralled down into the sea.

If she spoke, it was with a voice that made no sound; if there were sounds, they fell upon ears gone deaf; if she saw, it was with eyes longer capable of anything but selective sight; if she felt anything at all, it was with a disembodied

A SKULK OF FOXES

consciousness aware of nothing but the widening gap between the Life she had given up and what could become her Death.

One thought became paramount...

Just be quiet, Arabella...just be quiet and do your job...

And so she came to a far corner of the in-between, and all her senses returned to her in the realisation she finally had found the ones she had come to find...two shrouded forms that sheltered a dog-fox named Hasan and a vixen named Thelina...huddled in a wavering construct of the place where they had lived their lives together, beside a loom that wove Magick, and the splinters of stone chipped away to reveal the hidden beauty living there. She knelt to touch their shoulders, learned again how to cry when Zoraya turned an impossibly ancient face to her from the shelter of Gareth's arms, whose gingery hair had gone ghostly, and who wept at the tragedy of having to die in order to have his princess returned to him at all. She named them, softly, and they nodded, each reaching out a hand to one of hers.

Come with me she said, not recognising the voice that spoke the words. *I'll take you where you it's okay...*

Together they retraced her steps...or perhaps took a different path leading back to where Arabella wanted them to go, because now they encountered none of the hopelessness that had brought her to them, only a slow plodding sense of leaving in-between behind, and if there was no promise of celebration at the end of their odyssey, there was, at the very least, the knowledge that the numbness would somehow be taken away.

MICHAEL SUMMERLEIGH

They stood with their arms around each other, and Arabella's in turn round both of them, as they stood on the edge of the borderlands, not far from a great stone house that rose up like a sunrise upon the desolation they had left behind them. She heard a creaky voice and realised that Zoraya had called her name...was trying to say something to her...so faint and faraway that it could have been a breath of wind in another place and time. She shook her head, looked down into a face that still bore resemblance to the timeless beauty of the one she remembered from the day she had been born, giving her the gift of her daughter, and the dying sparks of gold in her eyes that now lived in her own.

"No, Zori...you mustn't...please don't...you had no way of knowing...

"None of us knew, no one of us ever dreamed of the things we would have t'do so we could just be with each other...the *family* that you and my mom and dad made so you could all be happy and safe...

"I know what's gonna happen t'me now. I can see all of it and I hate it because I know it can't be changed...but we've only done the best we could..."

She turned to Gareth, the face she remembered now drawn with lines that bore witness to what he had endured in order to be found having found his own beloved.

"You're not allowed," she whispered. "It doesn't serve any purpose now t'think about how things could've been different, so just hang on to Zori wherever you go... wherever it is that Love goes so it can go on you just hang on and don't let go..."

A SKULK OF FOXES

She lifted her head and nodded towards the stone house in the valley before them, that shone in sunlight and shadow, beckoning to them.

"That's where you need t'be right now," she said. "I can't take you back to where you should be…not anymore…"

Gareth said,"I shouldn't have done this to you…forced you—"

"You don't get to apologise either," she said. "You and Zori gave me 'Rissa. I know what's gonna happen, what it's gonna feel like, but it's still been worth something, and it still doesn't change anything. Just never let go of each other ever again…please promise…"

They nodded together, left the faintest touch of their lips on her cheeks.

"Teodor is in that house," she said. "Father Ambrosius. He knows everything now…he'll know where you should be going from here. I'm gonna go too. I wanna see my 'Rissa again…"

She heard the whispers of *Thank you I love you* from two voices growing more and more distant as the magick drew her back into the life that had belonged to her. They waved…turned…she watched them move slowly down a flower-strewn meadow followed by two foxes who kept close to their heels, and saw that Father Ambrosius was at his door waiting for them

She watched until she saw the round little man's arms around them, and went her way home…

…Stood in a courtyard no longer littered with the corpses of cats or apple trees or even the memory of the Chaos that had died there. She smiled at the shimmer on the other side—thought proudly *My mom made that*—and without any further thought stood before it...stepped through...turning... a brief offhand wave to scatter it away...turning again into a garret room at the top of a converted carriage house in St John's Mews...

...Slowly made her way went down one flight of stairs and then another leading down into the kitchen...where she heard voices... recognised each of them one by one and realised everyone who mattered was there. Halfway down that second stair three foxes wreathed her ankles and Yana leapt up into her arms.

You are safe...

She nodded, replied *Yes...safe, me...for now...you mustn't tell them... anyone... maybe I can still change it...*

All three nodded solemnly, and she smiled to see such a thing on faces that in the small time she had known them seemed always to smile. She came to the bottom of the stairs and stood in the doorway for a while, before 'Rissa looked up...

"You're home," was all she could say, rushing round the table...followed by everyone... her father limping a little bit...all of them crowding round to touch her she wondered if their hands might pass right through her...

"'Bella..." said Brandywine. She couldn't manage anything else, only stood before the mirror image of herself and fluttered her hands round her daughter's face.

'Bella said, "You did good, mum, real good...and I think we're done now. I think it's really over..."

Kerissa wouldn't let go...

"I found them, baby," she whispered. "I found them, and Hasan and Thelina was there too, and I got them all t'where they can be together...like us..."

Part Four

AT LAST

Chapter Twenty Seven – Bitter & Sweet

The summer passed slowly, in a delicious wave of warmth and sun. The lives that had been upended and sundered apart for a small while became whole again, and for them, the ones who had known the truth of the first sundering and paid the greatest price for their efforts, finally received its value back to them in days and nights that were long and full with everything they had ever wanted—peace, tranquility, the simple happiness that came from a family of their hearts.

One morning the sun came through the second floor windows of a Wyndham bedroom, rousing both Nicholas and Brandywine from sleep. They reached for each other in the same breath and found they'd never come apart from each other during the night; that his hand, that had rested on the curve of her hip, but had found its way into the tangle of curls between her thighs, had simply stayed there; that her arm, around his shoulders pressing him close up against her, had never left off until the moment of her waking, when her own hand strayed down his back and her fingers traced sleepy patterns amongst the hollows of his spine.

They said, "G'morning my love," in the same breath, and laughed for no reason at all.

A SKULK OF FOXES

"How's your leg today, Windy?" she asked, as she'd done every morning for most of the summer.

"It's fine, Branny," he replied slowly, still not fully awake, nor wanting to be just yet. "Yesterday was the first day it really didn't bother me at all, and this morning it's feels like it always felt, like before…"

His voice trailed off and his free hand went searching down one thigh to where a small scar had disappeared during the night, and the small sliver of his staff that Stella had thought to bring with from the other side, that Kerissa had slipped under the skin above the broken bone, was gone as well.

"I'll be racing through the Emerald Gardens by nightfall," he said, and wriggled round until she surrounded his face with warmth. "On second thought maybe I'll do that tomorrow," he said, though now his words were a bit muffled. He licked at her skin and she shivered.

"We're gonna be okay now, right?"

He nodded and licked again

"I'm afraid t'get lost in being too happy, Windy," she said to the top of his head. "I know it sounds silly because everything has been so wonderful ever since…but I've noticed things about 'Bella…not a lot…sometimes, though…when she thinks nobody's looking at her. Mostly she's just like when she was little…just like she used t'be, with 'Rissa and the twins and everyone else… but every now and then I see this look in her eyes…like when she came home last summer and was so unhappy…and all of a sudden I just wanna cry…"

Windy was silent, having seen those moments in his daughter every bit as clearly as Brandy.

"Maybe it's just going t'take some more time, Branny, " he said, hoping it was true. "Now that we've sold the studio on Old Princes and 'Rissa's come here t'live with us, it won't be long. All either of them has ever really wanted was t'be able t'be with each other all the time. You'll see...when they go off t'school together in the fall it will be some brand new good adventures for them to share."

"I hope so, but..."

Windy made question noises between her breasts.

"I heard them talking about that the other day. 'Bella said maybe she didn't want t'go."

Windy lifted his head and looked up into her eyes, saw himself mirrored in two emeralds that were close to tears...felt a wave of sadness that seemed to clog his throat. He forced himself to smile.

"They're together is all that matters, honey," he said...

※

"...It's different from with two girls," whispered Jamie knowingly, but nowhere near quietly enough.

Both Andrew and Alain became aware they were definitely *not* alone anymore. When they looked up, the twins were standing just inside the doorway of their bedroom and looking very attentive. Alain had the wackiest of thoughts that Stella was lacking only a clipboard and a pencil.

"When did you guys come in here?" asked Andrew. "We didn't hear a thing."

"You were busy," replied Jamie, "and Yana has been giving us *Quiet* lessons."

A SKULK OF FOXES

"Well you can tell Yana that they're working out just fine," grinned Alain.

Andrew looked at Jamie curiously.

"How d'you know it's different from with girls?"

Jamie looked slightly embarrassed.

"We seen 'Bella and Kerissa..." he said quietly, hoping it was the right answer.

"Really..."

"Not so many times..."

"Ysa says maybe she can teach us that disappearing thing," said Stella, trying to change the subject.

Andrew said,"You can tell Ysa that's not going t'happen."

The twins made faces.

Stella asked, "Is Jamie's gonna get big like that?"

Andrew sighed, reached for the sheet crumpled at the bottom of their bed and looked at Alain as if to say *They were your idea, y'know...*

Alain grinned again and said, "But you love them anyway, right?"

Andrew nodded in resignation, tossed his head to indicate that it was now acceptable for the twins to engage in their usual morning raid on their parents' bed.

"What's it like with a boy and a girl?" inquired Stella when they were settled in to everyone's satisfaction. "I know you get babies, but..."

Alain declined to offer the insights of his own experience, looked to Andrew as the source of the twins' illumination. In his turn, Andrew thought about it for a moment or two.

"Mostly it's the same shivery sort of good feeling," he said cautiously. "You guys will find out one way or the other eventually...but it's always best when you love the one you're with...then it's really special..."

"...'Bella...'Bella...could you stop for a minute I wanna talk t'you. It's important..."

Arabella stopped, lifted her head up and flung her arms around Kerissa's hips, put her chin on her belly and stuck her tongue in her navel.

"Okay don't stop just yet...but soon...really..."

Arabella nodded, which only served to make Kerissa's eyes go a bit blurry. Eventually she *did* stop, and looked up again with a big smile of satisfaction and smuggitude on her face.

"You taste very good this morning, my love," she said, with the air of one who knows exactly what it is they're talking about. Kerissa shook her eyes uncrossed.

"I'm not being unappreciative, but come up here and let me say..."

Arabella wriggled her way up the length of Kerissa's body, stopping briefly along the way, but eventually snugging herself comfortably where the chocolate girl could smooth hair from her face and plant kisses on her eyelids.

"Okay I'm ready now," she said, smiling with an abundance of impudence.

"I love you, 'Bella."

"Yeah you better," warned Arabella.

It was a time-honoured exchange that never failed to make them laugh, something from Arabella's first day at school when they were children, and she'd caught Kerissa ogling one of the boys in her class. Arabella had pretended to be huffy; Kerissa had offered a declaration of love to soothe her wounded whatever.

"What's up then?"

"I wanna go away for a bit...not long..."

Okay when are we going?"

"No, just me, 'Bella. I wanna look int'something and it's gotta be a secret squirrel for a little bit."

"I can't come with?"

Kerissa shook her and kissed her eyes again.

"Nope."

"You're sure?"

"Yep."

Arabella thought about it.

"I'm not happy."

"You'll get over it."

"Promise?"

"Sure."

"How long then...?"

"Three or four days...maybe five..."

"That's a long time, 'Rissa. You're gonna owe me..."

"I'm okay with that, 'Bella."

"When are you goin'?"

Kerissa shrugged and in doing so brought a nipple dangerously close to Arabella's lips.

"Soon. If I'm not here you'll know I'm off."

"Not now, though...?"

"No, 'Bella, not now..."

The blonde girl smiled and wriggled back to where she'd been.

"Okay..."

.

"...Ohhhhhhh no...I remember what happened the last time we did this."

"So do I," said Sebastian. "We were doing quite well until you took off with whoever it was you took off with."

"I didn't take off with anyone!" said Evrard. "I was abducted."

"Sure, Ev, whatever you say..."

"You're not being very respectful. I'm the king. If I say I was abducted then I was."

Sebastian said, "Sure, Ev, whatever you say..."

"I can have you thrown into the dungeons!"

"There aren't any dungeons anymore, Evrard. We flooded them and bricked 'em

up again. What else have you got?"

"I got a wire from your brother..."

"Oh...?"

"He said he's gonna be away a bit longer than planned...and he asked if it would all right if he moved to Bedford permanently."

"What'd you say?"

"I haven't said anything yet. I don't know why he's asking me in the first place."

"Well you're the king, after all."

"What's that got t'do with anything."

Sebastian laughed outright.

"Absolutely nothing. D'you think it's too early for breakfast?"

A SKULK OF FOXES

"I'm the king. We can have breakfast any damned time I want..."

"I was just checking...maybe in a little while."

"...Whatever you're doing, Tommy, is...well...it's really interesting," said Diana, stretching to where her toes touched the footboard of their bed.

"I'm not doing anything, Di," he said. "I'm lying here *thinking* about doing things, but I've not gotten round t'them yet..."

Her eyes shot open in less than a heartbeat, took in Thomas lying next to her with his eyes closed, and then looked over one shoulder at the dog-fox standing between them... with his tail doing a slow sarabande across one of the places that was rarely if ever unclothed in public.

"You little shit," she said.

Khalid grinned and disappeared.

"Tommy, d'you think maybe you could have a chat with the girls and ask them t'ask Khalid not to make unannounced appearances in our bedroom? They're the only ones he pays attention to these days..."

"I could do that," said Thomas. "What do I get for my trouble?"

She hit him with her pillow, levitated onto her stomach and draped one arm across his chest as she went nose-to-nose with his face.

"I think the question you *should* be asking is what you're *not* gonna get for putting that on the table."

"I see your point," replied Tom. "I'll get on it."

"Soon, please."

"Yesterday, my love."

Diana did some more stretching.

"Have we got everything together for the do on the weekend?" she asked.

"Alain said he'd have everything here tomorrow, Di. I don't think Edmund's still anywhere near home these days, but Sebastian said Evrard planned on disguising himself as a Scandian serving-wench so he could show up without anyone noticing."

"That should be interesting. He's pretty no matter which way he turns."

"Sebastian's been spending some time..."

"I know. I don't think they mean anything t'come of it, but Sebastian says they both just like being that close every now and again."

"He's not really said anythin t'me, Di..."

"Well I'm his mother."

Thomas sighed and rolled over to where Diana and he lay facing each other as opposed to her draped over top of him.

"One of these days you'll explain t'me how once upon a time all of us got into each other's knickers all the time, but now my younger son can only confide in his mother."

"Don't be an idiot, Tommy. He's trying to live up to some stupid idea that manly men don't talk about things like that with other men."

Thomas sighed.

"Well... I guess I'll just nurse my wounded whatever in silence then..."

A SKULK OF FOXES

"The hell you will," said Diana, shoving with both hands. Looking down at him,

she grinned. "I'm gonna *make* you make noise."

Thomas grinned back. "I was hoping for something like that..."

"G'morning, Mum..."

"G'morning 'Bella how are you?"

Brandywine turned away from washing breakfast dishes and then stopped, stared at her daughter.

"What?!?!?!"

Brandy shook her head and smiled.

"You're so beautiful. How on earth did that happen?"

Arabella made embarrassed faces.

"I'm pretty sure you and Daddy are the ones responsible...and then 'Rissa looked at me."

"Y'okay today?"

"I'm fine, Mum. Where *is* 'Rissa?"

"She said she was off on another one of her secret squirrels. Didn't the two of talk about it?"

"Not this one specific."

"Oh...well...she said she'd be back as quick as moonblinks so maybe it's just a couple of days."

"Mom, this is the third time...maybe even the fourth..."

"I know, sweetheart. She said she thinks she's almost where she wants t'be with it...a big surprise. D'you want some tea or coffee? I can make you some eggs for breakfast. Alain sent some over fresh last night..."

"Can I have tea...and maybe scrambles with some cheese...?"

"Toast too?"

Arabella nodded enthusiastically.

"That dark brown bread? With lots of butter?"

"Only if I get a hug first."

Brandywine got one that lasted a little bit longer than expected.

"You're sure you're okay?"

Arabella sighed and gave her mother a look of exasperation that ended with another hug.

"I'm fine, Mum. Really. You don't have t'be worryin' about me all the time."

"I'm your mom it's my job get used to it," said Brandywine.

"I saw Daddy upstairs, He said that *he* got a note from the gallery people and they want him t'make sure you're at the opening tomorrow night."

Brandywine looked huffy.

"They could've told *me* that! They're *my* paintings..."

"Yeah...but he's *the man of the house*..."

Brandywine made growling noises.

"'He laughed and said someday they'll find out you were in charge for twenty years and then they'll have a cow."

Brandywine looked puzzled for half a moment.

"I have no idea what that means."

"Me neither," said Arabella. "Must be from when he was growin' up with Grammy Alex and Grampa on the farm up north."

They laughed together, went to work on 'Bella's breakfast and eventually sat down at the long table together, both with mugs of tea and 'Bella with her cheesy scrambles and buttered toast.

"She'll be back soon, honey," said Brandywine quietly.

"I know."

"She misses you as much as you miss her."

"I know that too. Thank you so much for letting her come t'live with us."

Brandywine tilted her head to one side and looked puzzled again.

"Honey, Kerissa is every bit as important t'me as you are. Where else should she be? I don't even have thoughts where it's not *you and 'Rissa* t'gether in the same thought. And her mom and dad... Zori and Gareth..."

She stopped and looked away, clutched at her mug of tea so hard Arabella thought it would break in her hands...

"I'm gonna finish my breakfast, Mum. I think you should go upstairs and give Daddy a good reason not t'be workin' on that new sonata..."

A trice of foxes skulked in a corner of the back garden, noses to noses. A large grey tom-cat strode by secure in the inviolate nature of their relationship, but deigned to give them a regally feline nod of acknowledgment. Khalid made a rude noise.in his throat.

Is just teasing, him said Ysa.

Am teasing back replied Khalid.

Yana said *Is just a cat, not magical like us. Arabella would be upset.*

Also is very old added Ysa *and are not really knowing we if is magical or not, him...*

Yana made a fox-laugh.

Is gone again, Arabella he said.

Every time Kerissa is going said Yana.

Is nothing on the other side anymore. Following her once, me. Breaking all the gates, 'Bella is...

The three of them sighed together.

Maybe should be saying...one of us...? suggested Yana.

Ysa shook her head.

Is not for us like that to be in their middle...

Then what is for us? asked Khalid.

To be where they are needing when is time... replied Ysa ..*and not to be putting noses in places where belonging they are not...* she added pointedly.

<hr />

"...Hello my love I'm back!"

Kerissa bounded across Brandywine's small garret studio and wrapped her arms around Arabella, burrowing into the thick mass of her hair where she had pinned it up about her shoulders. The blonde girl turned into her arms, the sparks of gold in her eyes suddenly lit with an almost feverish brightness. Kerissa got down on her knees in front of her, looked up into her face, anxious... worried...

"Honey, what's wrong?"

"I missed you a lot, 'Rissa. I didn't like sleeping by myself at all. I'm so glad you're back please don't go away anymore."

Arabella's voice had become very small, like the little girl who used to cling to her older sister, before she had learned how to challenge the world. Kerissa managed to conjure her sunniest smile.

"I don't have to, 'Bella. I found what I was lookin' for, and whenever you feel like it I'm gonna take you there. No more secret squirrels."

"You promise?"

"I do," said Kerissa. "Cross my heart and hope t'die."

"Please don't say that!"

"What're you painting today?"

She turned and looked up at the canvas on the easel beside them...shivered...

" 'Bella, don't finish this one, okay? I promise never t'go away ever again just leave this one where it is or paint over it but don't finish it..."

Arabella put her head down, sliding off her stool until she was on the floor in Kerissa's arms again, her eyes closed, nodding and promising.

"'Rissa I don't think I wanna go t'school."

"But why, honey...think about all the boys we can tease....all the stuff you're gonna learn..."

Arabella shook her head; the pins in her hair came loose and it fell down her back, blazing in the sun coming through the skylight.

"I just don't wanna do it, 'Rissa. I can't think of anything I wanna learn there. Mom's showing me how t'paint properly, and Da's teaching me how t'play all his instruments. I guess I'm just afraid t'go."

She started crying, sobbing so hard her breathing stopped and started and wrenched her whole body so hard Kerissa had to hang on to her twice as hard to keep them both from being sprawled across the floor.

"You could go. I could come t'see you all the time."

"No way, 'Bella! I'm not goin' anywhere without you ever again. We'll figure out something t'do. We will. We've got forever..."

Arabella began to choke on her tears.

"I love you," said the blonde girl. "I love you forever so much."

"You better!" Kerissa said, and tried to sound like she was laughing...

Chapter Twenty Eight – Homecoming

It was somewhere in the month of Windfall, right in the middle between the end of summer and the beginning of autumn, when the trees began their yearly dream of winter sleep, to whisper of its imminence, contemplate a brief earthen rainbow display of colour before drowsing away into the grey of the winter to follow. The sky overhead was a pale blue, no longer blazingly white hot with the season past, nor quite the deepening shade brought on by sunlight travelling longer to reach those who lived and breathed beneath its shower of light.

Two young women on horseback cantered leisurely across the bridge spanning the Findhorn at Linden, already a slow day's journey north from the City. The fairer of the two, green-and-golden-eyed with a heavy fall of blonde curls down her back, sat a sleek chestnut mare; her companion, dark-skinned and amber-eyed with a bronze -and-copper halo of curls round her face, rode a stallion the colour that most nearly resembled the auric splendour of ancient whisky. Both wore earth-brown corduroy trousers tucked into the tops of knee-high boots of soft leather; both had put aside forest-green woolen ponchos in deference to the mildness of the weather, and rode in light blouses of bleached white linen. Beneath their discarded ponchos, now resting atop travelling packs tucked behind them, were double-daggered swordbelts and double-curved hunting bows, each with their own complement of hand-fletched arrows.

"You're not gonna tell me, are you," said Arabella, the fair-skinned one, pouting.

"Nope," said her companion, Kerissa, with an air of saucy smuggitude. "Not a word. You gotta trust me."

"You're bein' a poophead," said Arabella.

"But I'm *your* poophead, for as long as you've been alive, for this minute, and for every one of them that comes forever after, so you gotta go along with it," replied Kerissa.

She grinned, nudged her horse up closer to the mare and reached to stroke an inner thigh from knee to points north. Arabella sighed.

"That's not fair..." she said dreamily.

"I love you, 'Bella," said the dark-haired one. "I'm allowed."

They came off the bridge, and Kerissa immediately pointed her stallion's nose northwest, cross-country to where the low hills that lined the west bank of the Findhorn rose up between them and the Westvales. Arabella followed in her wake, gently urging the mare to keep up as the stallion took off in a joyous gallop. At the top of the first hill, Kerissa reined him in, turned to wait for her lover, morning sunlight darting into her hair to set it on fire.

"Please tell," said Arabella.

Kerissa shook her head.

"It's two more days, 'Bella. You gotta be patient."

"I don't wanna be patient anymore, 'Rissa. You've been off and gone almost half a dozen times since...you know...and it's all pretty mysterious if y'don't mind me saying."

A SKULK OF FOXES

Kerissa grinned again. "I don't mind you saying *anything*, 'Bella, but I get the *mysterious* from my mom and it shouldn't be a surprise, so..."

She shrugged. Arabella nudged *her* mount up close and leaned to kiss her, put her head down on her shoulder. Their horses stamped and made impatient horse noises, faced with an endless, beckoning expanse of hill and dale below.

"So I have t'promise t'behave?"

"Only while we're on horseback," replied the dark-haired girl. "Elsewise I'll be crushed if you don't *mis*behave."

She grinned a third time and urged them both down the hillside, out onto the rolling downs and leas on the edge of the Vales, that spread out in a widening arc to the west and north, on and on for league upon league of watered glens and forested grazing lands. Arabella rode a pace or two behind by design, so she could watch her love without having to explain how the end of travail and terror, this unhurried journey into Kerissa's *surprise*, already was fast become the best days of her life, a small freedom from the Antillian invasion, and all the heartache that had come with it.

She thought *Thank you for loving me... for always taking care of me...*

⁕

That second night they camped in an oasis of sorts, a stand of alder watered by an underground spring. It had been yet another brilliant day bathed in sunlight, clouds only daring a wisp or thought of themselves to mar the unbroken blue of the skies. Before sunset, Arabella brought down a partridge with her bow, and then had to force herself to contemplate dinner without first begging forgiveness and then making a promise. Not long after, Kerissa stripped her in firelight, seemingly to the amusement of their horses, and when the moon rose up over them, bringing the first real chill of the season, draped her in the magic warmth of a coverlet named *Equatoria* and knelt between her thighs. Dazed with lovemaking, Arabella wondered at the sweetness of herself in Kerissa's mouth, and made more silent, but-no-less heartfelt promises before they drifted off into sleep together.

Not long after starting out again the next morning, the dark-skinned girl stopped on the edge of another stand of trees and wrapped a silver ribbon round the trunk of the outermost of them. A few miles on, she did so again, this time round the bole of a towering maple. A dozen times more in the course of that morning's journey, she stopped to do the same.

"'Rissa...?"

"So we can find our way back?" she asked ingenuously.

Arabella shook her head, resigned to the *mysterious*...and then she realised they were being followed by a somewhat expansive pack of small four-footed creatures that, for a change, were not foxes. Curiosity compelled her to ask:

"Why are we being followed by all these cats?"

"Oh...?" said Kerissa archly. "I'd not noticed..."

Arabella spent the afternoon in a constant twist and wriggle in her saddle, as it became evident the pack was a great deal larger than she'd imagined at first. By evening it had become a small tide, that stood on the outskirts of the glade they'd chosen for the night, and silently bid them *sweet dreams*

A SKULK OF FOXES

before dashing off to a night-time forage for their own suppers. Arabella declined to string her bow, drank too much sweet red wine, ate bread and cheese, and was only half-awake when Kerissa's fingers shivered her off into sleep.

In the middle of the night she dreamt of being small again, with Kerissa's hand in hers, leading her through the Emerald Gardens, the animal park, in amongst all the enclosures where in one of them she imagined a skulk of foxes and a million kittens running around like loons and grinning because...somehow...the keepers couldn't keep track of them enough *not* to feed them all...

In the morning, Kerissa looked up at her over their mugs of tea, and said, "One more day, my love..."

One more day, to be spent in perfection, as if the world had been waiting for them, and had opened itself to them as a kind of reward and promise. They transferred all of Kerissa's things to the back of Arabella's mare, and she rode behind with her arms round Kerissa's waist and her head sleepy and content to just be taken away to wherever it was they were going. The Westvales unfolded before them on that third day, stopping only at noontide, in a village in the last stages of being rebuilt from the ground up.

"Swinton," said Kerissa. "The town Evrard's father burned before he and our boys caught up with him...before Sebastian took that knife in the chest..."

Arabella had never been there before, but strangely, Kerissa seemed to be warmly welcomed. She asked questions in a few quarters and received answers that seemed to please her. An older gentleman appeared to take a great interest in Arabella, but when she looked for him, to ask why, he was nowhere to be seen. They stayed for two hours past lunch, helping to raise a barn roof before taking to horse again. Arabella became impatient.

"No more ribbons?" she asked.

"No more," said Kerissa, shaking her head and smiling as they moved past the outskirts of the village. "I can find where we're going now, and we can always ask our way back in the other direction need be. Besides, these weans never get lost, even if they go walkabout for a few days at a time..."

The cats had become a small multitude in their wake.

Once again astride mare and stallion, they took a narrow cart track leading away from the village, that wound its way through fields showing the last summer growth before fall harvest—stands of poplar and maple, and open meadows filled with wildflowers that moved in no breeze at all as their feline army, having declined to invade Swinton, rejoined them, scurrying along to either side of the track, chasing after each other, leaping for butterflies, with swallows arrowing after small clouds of buzzing insects, and little grey-and-white chickadees masquerading as feathered rockets.

By early evening, they had left much of what passed for the signs of civilisation and settlement behind them, their horses moving at not much more than a walk as they sensed the end of their journey. The sun was just beginning to sink down into the evening, painting every outline of everything around them in a fiery blaze of colour. Below a ridge of low hills, Kerissa reined up in the long shadow of a massive outcropping of stone standing out from the one beside them. She took the reins of Arabella's mare and led them upward, along the far side, until they reached its crest, that wandered on westward until it became lost in heavy forest.

"Close your eyes now, 'Bella," she whispered.

The horses whickered softly. Arabella dutifully closed her eyes. They went on for the better portion of an hour, and she always tempted to sneak peeks, but bound by Kerissa's charge not to look. She felt their progress as a series of twists and turns through the forest, dipping her head whenever Kerissa warned her of a low-hanging bough. At length they came to a standstill, and she was given leave to open her eyes again...

...Looked down across a sloping hillside meadow, carpeted in lush grass and the last of the season's daisies and bluebells and black-eyed Susies—overlooking a vale wherein was nestled a small cottage in the crook of a meandering stream, with a thin ribbon of smoke curling up into the darkening sky from the fieldstone chimney that rose above the thatched roof.

From below came the sounds of a crowded garth-yard fenced roundabout the cottage—a handful of sheep, chickens, goats, a pair of milch-cows penned on the far side of a goodly-sized barn half hidden in a stand of trees on the far side of the stream. She thought *I know this place,* though she could not say how or why...

"'Rissa it's lovely," she whispered. "Where are we?"

'Rissa only smiled.

"Wherever we are it feels like we're expected, 'Bella, doesn't it...and just in time for supper too..."

MICHAEL SUMMERLEIGH

She nudged them down the hillside...slowly...as if each moment between them and their arrival at the cottage below was something precious, to be prolonged beyond the breath of its passage... savoured...the caress of a homecoming. Arabella had long since given over every aspect of their journey into the hands of her companion. Now she felt as if she were dreaming...lost in a cocoon of warmth, safe in something that sighed with infinite kindness. Kerissa whispered as they went down through the meadow with their four-footed retinue now warbling and chirping and mewing out loud.

"Remember t'tell your sister and brother you're not allowed t'chase them," she said, and 'Bella looked over to see the vixen Ysa now perched on Kerissa's saddle-bow. "They've come a long way, same as you." She turned and looked at Arabella. "One of the last things Grim wanted was for some of his folk t'have a new home...that the City had become a just a bit crowded as a result of their victory celebrations last year..."

Her face shone with a light that Arabella had never seen before.

"'Rissa what's goin' on? You gotta tell me...now...please...where are we? Why did you you bring me here?"

Kerissa shook her head.

"Not just yet, baby. Minutes away...but what I *can* tell you...so I'm not spoilin' *all* of the surprises...is that I'd never known of this place before we thundered off into nowhere to rescue my da. I know you went to some dreadful places because you were the only one...the *only* one who could go there...but for starters I ended up here...so after it was all over... this time once and for all I hope...I wandered off t'find it...for us. I didn't know *why* it was important, but I knew it was..."

They were halfway down the hillside when the door of the cottage opened and a tall figure stepped into the garth-yard, shaded his eyes against a stab of sunlight and waved, before turning back into the doorway for a moment. Seconds later, Arabella saw yet another, but-not-*quite*-so-tall shadow in the doorway, standing close to the first one, and then three more besides, much smaller.

"'Rissa, isn't that Edmund?"

"It is, my love."

"Who're all the others please tell me."

"'Bella, the one cozied up next to Edmund is Darya...Robin's wife...you remember her, don't you? Edmund took her back to Bedford after that dreadful day and...and the others are her children. I asked them t'come here and make this place ready for you."

"Ready for *me*? 'Rissa, I don't understand."

"I promise you will, 'Bella...I promise..."

Edmund and Darya met them at the garth-gate, smiling, arms round each other, the children trailing behind, shy with the prospect of meeting creatures out of mythology and legend, and suddenly in complete awe as they saw Ysa on Kerissa's saddle-bow, and then noticed the horde of cats keeking out from the grass surrounding the stead. The young women slipped from their saddles, 'Rissa stroking Edmund's face making silent *thank yous* as he readied himself for Arabella's leap into his arms. Muffled up in her embrace he somehow managed to introduce the children—the twin girls Devon and Daryl, and younger brother Daniel—before asking them to look after their guests' horses. He lowered Arabella to the ground; she turned to Darya, trying to find some words...

"I know," said the Bedford wife. "Whatever it is, 'Bella...I know. Thank you so much for saving him...my Robin...and your mother...somehow...for this one...coming to save *me*..."

Edmund at last got his due welcome from 'Rissa, arm in arm following as Darya and Arabella led them into the cottage. A small fire blazed beneath their supper on the hearth. Ysa came indoors a step behind them all, raced for the warmth of the hearthstones and curled up there, her muzzle comfortably nestled down on her forepaws, contentment in the glint of her black button-eyes. While no one was looking, Khalid and Yana did a slow shimmer into existence beside her.

Dinner was a thick chicken soup full of rice and garden vegetables, fresh-baked dark bread redolent with molasses, and endless mugs of ale from a keg imported *en route* over a week before from Taunton, when Edmund and Darya had arrived from the west in response to Kerissa's request to *make things ready*. That it had come in the form of a magical unspoken message from a not-there-a-second-ago fox had served only to the make the children frantic with anticipation.

Arabella and 'Rissa found themselves the object of their unshakable attention, their excitement contained only so long as it took Daniel, the youngest, to climb up into 'Bella's lap and claim her as his own; Devon and Daryl took possession of Kerissa, mesmerised by the glow of her eyes and the deep warm chocolate-colour of her skin. Edmund and Darya looked on from beside the small hearthfire, radiating a warmth of their own that only added to the welcome Arabella and Kerissa had received upon their arrival.

"Edmund talks to these foxes," said Daniel to Arabella. "We heard them too."

Kerissa looked down at her two new charges and arched an eyebrow or two.

"We did," they said together; then Daryl spoke for both of them. "Edmund says they're magical and we're going to the City and we're going t'meet lots of new people and someone named Annie Branny..."

"That's Arabella's mom," said Kerissa.

"Is she magic, too?"

"I think when we get there we're going t'find magic everywhere," said Darya, putting her head on Edmund's chest. She smiled drowsily, looking at her guests. "I hope it's okay I'm stealing him..."

"You're not stealing him at all," said Arabella. "You're just coming home, is all...after some bad times." She looked down at Daniel and then at the the girls. "You're da was a hero, y'know, one of the bravest kindest persons I've ever known..."

They looked proud.

"I've got t'report back to Ev," said Edmund, "but I didn't think he'd mind if I came east again on my own time and brought company with. If he gets huffy about it...well...it's his own damn fault for sendin' me in the first place...though I'm not sure how he's gonna feel about me just up and going back t'Bedford t'learn how t'be a fisherman."

He shrugged and grinned, and wrapped Darya up in a hug to where she seemed to get lost in his arms without any second thoughts.

"Mom says da was friends with the king, too," said Daniel. "Is that good?"

"It's better than good, Daniel," said Kerissa. "You'll all get to meet him yourselves...but right now you're all lookin' sleepy so how 'bout I tuck you in and your mom and Edmund can come up for a goodnight?"

She trooped them up into the loft, followed by a trice of foxes bent on some last-minute mischief. 'Bella got curious again, obvious enough that Darya explained:

"When you found out that Robin had died, I realised how much he'd meant t'you, that for all it was only the span of a day you ever spent together, you were like a pair of old souls found each other again at last...

"Your mom took me t'the palace the next day... the one after we met so briefly, and I began to understand that something I'd never even dreamed of had happened...for all of us...that it was magic I suppose, whatever *that* is, *I* certainly don't know...except that all of a sudden I did, because Edmund brought me back to my children...Robin's children...and it felt like he was always meant t'do that...t'come along and turn away the hurt of having lost him...that what they'd done together along with the king—?"

"Evrard," Arabella said softly. "You'll meet Diana, Edmund's mum, in the City. She still calls him *the brat from the Dales*. Next time you see him I think he'd be pleased no end if you were t'think of him as your brat as well. He's really just a little bit older than me, y'know..."

"The children can't wait," said Darya. "They've never been..."

A SKULK OF FOXES

Arabella smiled, looked upwards into the loft where they could hear giggling over the yips and squeaks of three foxes. Kerissa came down the stairs a few minutes later.

"You'll be goin' on then," she said.

Edmund nodded.

"First light tomorrow," he said. "We've got invitations to deliver, and you two should have some time t'yourselves just now, so we're gonna go on up and keep the kids company. There's blankets and pillows and you can kick up the fire if it gets too cold..."

When they were gone upstairs, 'Bella turned to Kerissa.

"Invitations?"

Kerissa nodded. "We're hosting a handfasting, my love...here...at Yuletide... with the fall season for a bunch of folk from Taunton and Swinton t'come in and build us a proper guest house for *everyone* coming...from the City and up north and our whole family together...safe...finally..."

"Rissa your mum and da—"

"It's okay. I don't worry about them anymore, 'Bella. You said they'd be okay wherever it is you brought them, so they're together now, along with Hasan and Thelina... It's okay for *us* t'go on."

"Not until you explain."

Kerissa nodded.

"Starting right now, my love," she said, dragging their bed-linen and blankets from a corner so they could lie down in front of the fire.

KERISSA'S STORY

MICHAEL SUMMERLEIGH

"...I'd seen this place, 'Bella. And because me and you and your da was on the other side for a while, what I saw made me curious. When I found it for real I learned a little treasure that I'll share in a little while. In the middle was when we all were back and safe and I wandered off like you said...

"I didn't know where I was supposed t'go, so I just followed my nose...or wherever my pony decided t'take me on any given day...and I ended up in a place that Edmund and Sebastian and Evrard had talked about...Swinton...

"I wasn't even really paying any kind of attention, but all of a sudden I was in the middle of lots of stuff going on...people who had just put the roof on the brand new inn...and it felt like half the people of the village were sittin' round the fire in what was t'be the common room, still open to the wind because they'd not yet gotten round to the walls... but I started describing the very same thing you saw when I said it was okay t'open your eyes again, 'Bella, and this older gentleman in a corner suddenly perks up from where I thought he'd just ponked out after the day's work. He started lookin' at me really close like. I could see him out the corner of my eye...that he was holdin' back from comin' over t'talk t'me until the place started to empty out a bit. Then he roused himself up, sat down at one of the empty tables, and called out if I'd be good enough to humour an old man and join him...

When I'd sat down beside him he introduced himself as the miller of Swinton until the mill had been burnt down just before harvest the year before.

"...Some bastard from up in the Dales come through here and just burned us out for sport..."

A SKULK OF FOXES

He ordered a whisky for himself and told the taverner to give me another of whatever I'd been drinking...and then he asked me how I knew about this place..."

"...What place are we talking about?" I asked, not so much mistrustful of him, but just being cautious...

"The one you're talkin' about, young miss," he'd said. *"A place I know pretty well though it's well off the beaten track, and mostly unknown, even for most of the people now livin' here in Swinton."*

"It's real? You know where it is?"

"Of course it's real," he'd said, nodding as the barkeeper delivered his whisky and my cup of mead, *"and I know exactly where it's at...less than a day's ride from here...but I need t'know why yer askin' over it, miss, because it's a place of a great heartache for me that knows of it, and remembers it from when it was new."*

"I told him I'd seen it in a dream, and his eyes got real wide at that, 'Bella, like maybe I was some kind of loon for dreaming of a place I'd never seen, nor even knew about...but I told him that after I was all finished up with dreaming about this place, it just seemed really important that I should find it...that I'd know why once it was found. I could see he was suspicious of me, not in an unkind way and I didn't blame him at all because he was just bein' wary of givin' away something to a total stranger that was important to him...an outsider...and then I told him everything that Edmund and Sebastian and Evrard had told us about the night they came here after Ev's father...that *they* were part of our family...and that's when I think he started t'trust me with his story..."

THE MILLER'S TALE

"It was a long time ago, almost forty years. I was just then maybe twenty-years old, and as my father had died the summer before I'd taken over runnin' the mill, because it was our family's callin' here for over three generations.

"A young man my age or so at the time come down from some place far up past the Dales that summer, all blonde and blue-eyed like from some Scandian family, maybe the fifth or sixth son of his father, and so without any kind of prospects for himself that wouldn't go to his older brothers first. His name was Jacob, and with the mill being on the north side of the village it was what he come to first, where I was, and we became fast friends, him takin' up with me t'run the place...

"I had me a local girl then. You'd not know it now t'look at me, but then I was a fair dash of a fellow amongst the young lads here, and Molly was the fairest dash of a may in our corner of the Westvales, with hair the colour of gold in the sun, and big green eyes t'go with. We was sweethearts, had been so for the better part of a year, but then, after only as long as it took that first summer t'go by and her t'take notice of my new friend Jacob, she cried a bit and said goodbye t'me.

"All the others boys round here was at me t'thrash the daylights out of 'im for stealin' my girl, but y'had t'know Jacob t'realise he'd never meant t'do me any kind of mischief... that it was Molly herself who'd gone so sweet on *him*, and her bein' the way she was, in the end all I could do was wish her and Jake the best. There was lots of other girls for me, maybe no quite the beauty that Molly was, but I was never lonely t'the account of her *or* Jacob so I got over the hurt and stayed friends with 'em both...close friends...close enough that when they was married I stood for Jacob and helped them to find the place you seen in your dream...

A SKULK OF FOXES

"We built their cottage together, in a glen we'd discovered whilst out ramblin' about the district, a place even I'd not seen before, hidden away from the world as it were, this little paradise of a place that nobody else seemed t'know was there. The rush of clean vales water that washed round it come from a spring out the earth about a half mile away, and then went under the ground after another half mile or so t'join up with one of the other streams in the region that fed the Findhorn farther east, so there was nowt t'lead anyone there by design.

"Away they went for that fall and winter, and come the next spring I wondered that they'd not come int' Swinton for anything in most of that time. Well int'the summer I went out there, thinkin' that Molly had been expectin' almost right away after they was wed and it was a strange unsettling thing not t'have seen nor heard of them since the Yuletide.

"I found them together in their bed, arms round what was left of each other with the critters havin' gotten to 'em, and no sign of any child ever havin' been born there at all…"

Kerissa wriggled her way between Arabella's legs, pressing herself up close to her in the wash of moon- and starlight that stole in from the night. There were odd rustlings and scurryings in the air outside the cottage, and the squeaks of mice and whatever else out foraging with the less-than-good-fortune to encounter the new feline residents.

"And that was that," she whispered, nuzzling into the linen of Arabella's blouse to find a comfortable place between her breasts. "The next morning he brought me here, said the place hadn't been lived in for all the time since; that he buried his friend and lost love and then went back t'Swinton, tellin' anyone who asked that they were dead, and the place where he'd thought t'have left them the year before was haunted...full of things you'd never ever want t'meet in day or night..."

"'Rissa I still don't understand," murmured Arabella. "You said Edmund and Darya had come here t'put this place t'rights for *me*."

Kerissa looked up and nodded.

"One last little mystery, my love," she said. "Come with me..."

Arms round her girl's waist, Kerissa eased her up from beside the fire and took her hand, leading her out into the garth-yard and through the gate and then down towards the stand of willows that stood in the curve of the stream that shimmered silver in the moonlight. At the water's edge she turned them round and pointed to a sheltered place between two of the trees, and a broad flat stone set into the ground there....words crudely chiselled into the flat surface.

Kerissa drew her closer, knelt with her so they could read the simple inscription:

Jacob and Molly Lloyd
for always...

"This is *your* place, 'Bella. Our place now. This is where your mum was born, baby. Jake and Molly were your other grandparents..."

Arabella's hand tightened round Kerissa's, her eyes glistening in the moonlight.

"Does my mum know?"

A SKULK OF FOXES

Kerissa grinned and kissed her mouth. "I thought it could be a surprise for Yuletide... when everybody's here for Edmund and Darya's handfasting..."

Epilogue

AMARANTHUS

My name is Arabella Wyndham, the only child of Nicholas Wyndham, the famous composer whose name I bear, and Brandywine Lloyd, whose likeness I share, who was a wonderful artist and for twenty years was the Queen even though nobody ever knew. I live alone now, though my little valley is home to dozens of cats, and likely an equal number of foxes, and an awful lot of them seem t'just wink in and out of the world without a second thought. They all sleep in my bed and in the rafters of my house; in the winter months they fill the barn and the guest house. The foxes have been told they musn't ever chase the cats, so the cats in turn go bravely about their business with a smug sense of their superiority. I sometimes think they're really the only things in my life that can make me smile anymore.

We all had a few years of being free from people...things...intruding...bringing grief and trouble into our lives. We saw each other, visited each other constantly, and we got t'where we stopped being afraid to laugh too loudly or be too happy. One day Evrard the new King came to visit and stayed for a few days. Me and 'Rissa still remembered the first time we'd met him...how we teased him all the time...

A SKULK OF FOXES

We did that all over again, and we sent his small entourage off t'Swinton to enjoy themselves so we could enjoy *our*selves...

The story was supposed t'be that Kerissa died giving birth to Evrard's son, Gareth de Montigny, so she could be stop being the queen of our country and come back here to be with me; but the story turned out to be no story at all, just one more caution to prove there's a price to be paid for everything...consequences...especially if you do Magick. She did come home to me at last, but she's sleeping now as she's slept ever since that day, in the stand of cypress on the banks of my little stream, in company with my mom and my dad and their parents, and everyone else I've ever loved. I talk to her...I talk t'them all... every day...and there are times when I'll sit there for days at a time, and then the foxes and the cats know they have t'forage for themselves for a while. They always come to sit with me, so I know the sound of cat-and-fox sorrow as well as I know my own. I think I would die without them, or so I tell myself, becoming more and more certain as the years go by that this will *never* be the case because I'm pretty sure I can't die...

Consequences. An act of Love by a Nubian princess seemingly raised from the dead; one last sacrifice in the wake of heroic effort...to give me back to her daughter. And a few nights, spent with a boy from the Dales who my mom made king... a few nights for the fun and sheer joy of being young together and at peace with the world... finally. A few nights that ended up taking 'Rissa away from me.

Even then, before she died, I think what we shared had begun to change a little bit. Both of us noticed. As time went by, even before our play-time with Evrard, it became obvious that the little girl who had claimed me as her own, and swore to take care of me forever, had sort of become *my* child, and it became my part to look after her. I could never explain the way I felt...that *I* had changed...that *I* was changing... There were nights when we would leave off making love to each other and just hang on, in tears, for no reason that made any sense to either of us.

Consequences. They're everywhere, whether you recognise them or not. My mother gave Magick away to Zoraya so she could save us all. Then she gave it away one last time, thinking that over the centuries Magick had done as much harm as good, and to our corner of the world especially. And then Zori chose to give herself in return for my life...a parting gift to her own daughter that set in motion...again...another bunch of things that became more than my portion of that gift, given in Love...ending in heartache.

Consequences. To me they're the constant companion of my solitude. I'm the only one left. I watched my mum and my da grow old and die. I watched them mourn the passing of his parents, who welcomed my mother to their family as if she were one of their own. I've watched over Edmund and Sebastian and comforted them when Diana and Tom grew old; watched my sweet uncles Alain and Andrew...the twins...who married into Edmund and Darya's family, her own children with Robin and one son of their own whom they named Nicholas, after my father. I watched them grow. I watched them live their lives in peace and make more of us...Evrard to give over the kingdom to my 'Rissa's baby boy... and I watched them all die.

A SKULK OF FOXES

Zoraya just wanted her daughter to have me back in her arms, to love me and let me love her for the rest of our lives. For all her wisdom, for all her knowledge of the secrets and mysteries of the universe, she let Love hide away a true understanding of the meaning of *consequences*.

They're all gone. Everyone I've ever known and truly loved...gone...and as long as they lived, even when we breathed sighs of relief that the bad things were over, there wasn't a day when consequences failed to haunt all of us, tinge the laughter and simple joys of our lives in one way or another with bittersweet knowledge of loss, and the price we all pay for what each and every one of us poor living things should always have as our due...

Over time I've tried t'find them on the other side, living different lives perhaps, but alive...somewhere. Along my way, never finding them, I've smashed every gate I ever encountered, knowing all along what would happen, because in becoming what I am, in the effort to save my family, I saw all of the hundreds and thousands of lives I could live, and as well, I saw the one life I was living and what it would come to.

So many times I've been tempted to make new doors to go back into the whirlwind source of Existence, to try one more time...see if *I* could magick my loved ones back to me...and then I would remember that there were always consequences... always...even with the best of intentions, and that we need to be very cautious with the things we wish for...the things we dream about...

I have a great black draft horse in my stable, perhaps the last of a line that began in the Carillon, with my father as a small boy bouncing along on a small mountain named

MICHAEL SUMMERLEIGH

Amadeus...and then 'Rissa and me on his son, Diomede...and at least half a dozen others since...

Once or twice a year I ride Hasan into one of the towns a day's ride from my valley. I've been doing it for so long I don't think anyone has ever really lived long enough to notice that I've never grown in anything but years; that I'm the same Arabella who came back from the dead on a day in early summer, washed ashore naked as the day I was born, a few days shy of my eighteenth birthday.

Sometimes they find me in my hidden valley, come asking for some charm or favour. Mostly they just stay away, leave gifts somewhere along the way, with notes asking for this or that. The ones that find me I turn away with a smile and a *glamour*, so they'll never know it was me cured their ills, brought them love or a good harvest. I try t'be careful, knowing nothing is for certain, that everything can always go wrong in some way or another...and I never mess with Death. Death is a Mystery, and some mysteries are bigger than Magick because there's no rhyme or reason to any of them, no laws that say when and where. They just are...and so I'm *always* careful...

...And try t'be mindful of consequences, since I've become one myself. I know where it all began—with the beautiful young orphan girl who was my mother, and the boy she loved who was my father...and the goodness in their hearts that compelled them to try to lessen the burdens of a queen named Caroline de Montigny...take away the weight of her loneliness and exhaustion. I've learned of both.

My mum always said that when we die we go back to where we come from...get stirred up in the universe and come back again. I'm still waiting for everyone to come back to me. I don't dare cry for them, because if I do I don't think I could ever stop...

But I wear 'Rissa's moonstone on my left hand and I've noticed that as the years have gone by it's starting to darken a little bit...

So my name is Arabella and now *I'm* the unfading flower...but maybe not forever. Maybe if I'm quiet and just do my job...

Milton Keynes UK
Ingram Content Group UK Ltd.
UKHW021001241024
450188UK00012B/532